GOOSE AND THE OCELOT

A FUC ACADEMY STORY

RENEE HEWETT

FOREWORD

A note from Eve Langlais…

Renee Hewett, whose secret identity also happens to be my very awesome assistant, is the reason I decided to open up my worlds. She and I had many conversations about how we could handle it. When I expressed doubt about anyone wanting to actually write in my worlds, she smacked me! For real. LOL. Okay, she didn't slap me, but she did encourage me to not be afraid. To relax, sit back, and see what amazing stories others might have to give. If this whole world thing works, then she deserves most of the credit.

She is an epic friend, an excellent assistant, and as you're about to discover, a gifted writer.

Please show her some love. And no you can't have her.

She's mine. All mine. Don't make me lick her, she might quit if I do!

Happy reading, and giggles,

~Eve

ACKNOWLEDGMENTS

Eve, I can't believe this is happening!

I'm not very good at saying this often enough, but I know just how lucky I am to consider you a friend, and to have you in my life. I've learned so much from you and you inspire me so damn much (maybe I should say "so fucking much," that's probably more appropriate), and I can't believe that you're opening your world and letting people like me into it!

Thank you. Thank you. *Thank you.* Never doubt that you're the best.

I also need to thank the other local world authors who were brave enough to do this too! Mandy

Rosko, Alexa Gregory, Jenn Burke, Lucy Farago, TB Mann, and Jodi Kendrick: thank you for all the write-ins and brainstorming sessions. Thanks for humoring me while I read you my newest line or acronym that was amusing me.

Rebecca Poole, I love my cover, I can't believe it's mine! Thank you for being a fantastic designer to work with, and for also being someone I consider a friend!

Jessica Snyder and Devin Govaere, you two are the best, for real. I couldn't do this without your help. Thank you for encouraging me and making me a better writer. Thank you Anne Victory and Crystalle Berry for the final eyes.

And finally, thank you to my family and friends for supporting me. I love you all!

~Renee Hewett

Andrés Sosa prowled through the dense forest. He was at home leaping gracefully from tree limb to tree limb, despite the tangled vegetation and heavy humidity.

The tropical climate felt right to him. It was warm and thick, and something others might complain about, but not Andrés. He was a native to Brazil and felt much more comfortable there than in the cold Canadian winters. Hell, if matters weren't so dire, he might just think about taking his time finding his target so he could escape the frigid north even longer.

But a good FUC agent didn't dillydally. Especially knowing the likes of Mason and Viktor were keeping a close eye on the clock. Andrés wouldn't live it down if he took too long and failed to make the top agent retrieval time.

So he'd skipped the pool bar and gotten straight to work. Dedra Wakins' daughter had been plenty cooperative in providing information on where her mother was staying, but when Andrés arrived at the swanky resort, he found that she'd already bolted. Had left on a river cruise with a much younger man.

The goose was a cougar.

The boat rental clerk's tongue didn't wag until Andrés came up with the right amount of green. When he did, she tucked it away in her shirt and then admitted that they had trackers on their boats, a way to ensure tourists didn't go missing or try to make off with their assets.

Andrés used the FUC tablet blessed by Jessie, their very own black swan tech genius, to tap into the tracking system. He saw that Dedra and her boy toy had a bit of a lead on him, so he abandoned the idea of renting a boat and instead headed into the jungle on foot, where, when out of sight from other people, he shifted.

He'd be able to catch up with them much more quickly as a tree-leaping ocelot.

Birds flew off in a panic at the sight of the

dangerous cat. He was a magnificent golden creature, with solid black spots and stripes covering his body and the softest round ears, which enabled him to look adorable if he needed to. It also helped with the ladies.

His kind wasn't as large as the other wild "big cats," but he challenged anyone who dared call him small. He preferred the term "compact" and would prove that his kind could measure up to any "big cat," like lions and tigers. Most often, though, he was compared to a cheetah because of the similar coloring. Cheetahs were bigger and could beat an ocelot in a race over open savannah, but they'd be left in his dust here in the jungle.

Birds squawked and chirped and flew away from him. Snakes and other reptiles clung to branches and glared. The creatures could thank Lady Luck today, though, because this kitty wasn't there to play. He was on a FUC mission, with one specific fowl in his sights.

FUC was the Furry United Coalition, the shifter agency that guarded and protected their own, and their secrets, from threats from the outside world. This was Andrés' first field assignment in a while since he'd taken a teaching position at the new FUC newbie academy, that was FUCN'A for the uninitiated. He'd taken this job because it was a mission that required his very specific set of skills.

Or just because he wanted the excuse to vacation to South America.

Who could say?

He was the top agent most comfortable in South America, who could fly a plane, and who could also sweet-talk the goose if she refused to cooperate.

Andrés Sosa fit the bill. He was the best. Sure, they might all say that, but put any bear, bunny, or croc in this jungle with him and he'd find their prey and lap them over a few times before they inevitably crawled to him asking for help.

Because this was Andrés' turf.

And he proved it by finding his target even quicker than he'd estimated he could. It was simple, really. He'd followed the river and made easy use of the tallest trees to move much faster than their boat. It was the first and only one he saw, and he knew it was the correct one because he immediately recognized Dedra on board.

Platinum blonde, clad in only a bikini and netted covering—that really barely covered anything—and exuding the kind of confidence that only a mob princess and corporate heiress could, Dedra Wakins was the kind of woman Andrés usually didn't bother with.

Typically, that kind of woman eschewed adventure and preferred to enjoy a more sterile life. But he had to wonder if his assumptions were wrong, because here Dedra had chosen to leave home and vacation at a resort by a jungle and gone out on a cruise with what appeared to be no wait staff.

Bold! Who would prepare lunch?

The boat was moving at a languid pace, which gave Andrés some time to mull over what he should do. Take a flying leap onto the boat, shift, introduce himself, and then politely tell Dedra that he was there to return her to her home country?

He didn't like the idea of his stick and balls waving freely in the wind as he stood nude and unarmed between the goose and her paramour.

So then, should he stick to the shore? Shift and shout that she needed to go with him if she wanted to live?

Nah, they'd just ignore the ramblings of a random naked jungle man.

And forget trying to get his message across to her in shifter form. It didn't matter how precise his signing was. People never looked past the fur to understand his message. Or so he told himself.

Clarice simply said it was that sign language didn't work without opposable thumbs.

As he was trying to develop a plan, he noticed something odd about the lovebirds. They didn't seem as cozy as he would have expected.

Dedra didn't lounge back in the bow cockpit, with one arm resting on the side while the other held on to a martini. She wasn't enjoying a tanning oil massage from her young companion—something Andrés rather enjoyed imagining, but only if he were the one with the oil. No, she was sitting quite stiffly with her arms behind her—likely tied—while the man paced in front of her, gesturing wildly and seeming to be ranting.

Andrés made his way closer, prowling on the sturdiest of branches, the ones that wouldn't bend too much under his weight. Was this some kind of kinky game they were playing? If so, maybe he could get a jump on them both while they were distracted.

The man inside the beast growled at that. Something was wrong here, and it wasn't just some macho jealousy at not wanting that runt's hands on a woman like Dedra. Sure, only one look was enough to tell him that she was one hell of a tasty goose. Enough that Andrés wanted to hop into that boat and offer to show her how a man her age could rock her world in a way that the inexperienced youngster couldn't dream of.

But he was pretty sure they weren't playing. He wasn't reading distress from Dedra's body language, but she also didn't look like she was enjoying herself.

Had his target been captured by someone else?

Even better! He'd spring down, shift, take out peewee—the other man—and then let Dedra beg to have her way with Andrés' peewee—better known as Maximus. He'd have to turn her down, of course. He adhered to a strict rule of needing to finish the mission before there could be any celebration. Once they were back in Canada, and he was released from FUC duty, then all bets were off.

And then he saw that the man held a gun.

Fuck. Things had just gotten serious.

The little shit who had her wasn't one of the ones profiled in the mission files. Was it possible that his goose had more enemies?

Sure, it was possible. She was a mob princess, after all. She probably lived her life in danger of one sort or another. This was just the first time FUC had gotten involved.

He observed her now, captivated. She never showed she was ruffled, no matter how spitting mad the young man got—literally. Andrés could see the

7

droplets from where he crouched. She didn't fight back or try to escape but made sure to be continually facing him, rotating any time he paced from one side to the other of the pontoon boat. Andrés hoped that meant that this guy wasn't the sort who would shoot someone who was looking right at him, but the kind of chicken who could only shoot someone in the back.

Because that meant that Dedra was keeping herself safe.

As Andrés followed the riverboat, he was able to catch bits of the conversation. It seemed like his speculation that this had something to do with Dedra's late father's mob practices was not it at all. This wasn't about something Dedra's daddy had done.

It was something Dedra had done to this guy's daddy.

Andrés' goose was already cooked. Or at least, halfway cooked. Tied, anyway.

At this point, Dedra was starting to get bored. She'd thought the faux-kidnapping might be an exciting diversion from her otherwise mundane travels, but the longer Creed Maassen droned on about how Big Daddy Rod had left him no inheritance, the more annoyed Dedra got.

When he'd first approached her, pretending to be a stranger, Dedra had played along, curious to see what he was up to. She was only a few weeks into her southern migration, and she was already finding it dull. There was little to do, and few people who offered company she enjoyed, but she certainly wasn't going to cut it short and go back home, not so long as lady winter was keeping the place on ice. She'd long since outgrown her willingness to shovel snow and scrape ice from her windshield, but unfortunately, she'd also outgrown the appeal of partying into the wee hours of the night with random strangers. She was too old for that shit.

What she really wanted was her family to be there with her. How much fun it would be to lounge with Kailee on the beach or race her brother in laps around the pool. What she wouldn't give for her mother and father to be back among the living so they could indulge in extravagant meals and night-time shows.

But her kid was off doing her own thing, too busy for a winter vacation. Her brother and his kid didn't migrate anymore. And her parents had passed on this past year, just as her husband had ten years ago.

She envied the goose families that had flocks of family to turn to.

Hers had always been, unfortunately, small, without a brood of aunts, uncles, and cousins. It was likely because her father kept most people away. The better to make sure family secrets never got out.

Which meant that now Dedra wintered alone and found that solo vacations were kind of a bummer.

So she'd followed Creed to the boat and acted surprised when he "revealed" who he was. He'd thought that a flimsy attempt at a disguise and the fact that she'd never met him in person before would be enough to hide who he was. But he hadn't known that Dedra happened to be great at seeing through disguises, and Creed had an unmistakable resemblance to his progenitor.

She'd gone along with letting him zip-tie her hands behind her back and acted passively as the boat floated through the jungle. She allowed herself to enjoy the scenery and even thought back to the few times she'd been actually kidnapped as a child.

The code meant kids were supposed to be left alone, but sometimes people got desperate. At least they'd always been kind to her and her brother. She rather liked the time they were held in a warehouse and allowed to eat all the candy they wanted while watching *Gilligan's Island*.

It all amounted to Dedra having a—probably unhealthy—lack of fear in dire situations.

Because things always worked out.

She gazed into the water while Creed busied himself for a moment with the boat's controls. She wondered what kind of goose-eating monsters might be in the river, because it was looking to be the perfect time to go for a swim.

Dedra's tolerance for this little shit's whining was depleted.

"Mine! It was all mine!" He came back toward her, voice shrill, still waving the gun around. "And then he dies, and I come to find out he was *broke?* Do you have *nothing* to say for yourself?"

Dedra shook her head. She wouldn't bother trying to rationally explain to the nitwit that he should have taken a closer look into Big Daddy Rod's past before jumping to the stupid conclusion that Daddy's most recent ex was the problem. Sure, she understood how it seemed like the most reasonable explanation, that the best person to blame for the lack of fortune was some gold-digging slut—his words, not hers. Dedra enjoyed sex just fine and would never try to label or shame someone for it.

Dedra thought it was a shame that a son couldn't imagine any other reason why a hot number like Dedra would have been with Rod. Didn't he hear the way women purred when they said his name? *Big Daddy Roddd...*

But all of that was beside the point. There were two enormous reasons that Dedra would never worry about Creed's accusations.

First, Dedra was rich as hell. Monstrously rich. Billionaire rich. The Masseen's fortune would be less than a drop in the bucket for her—not worth the time and energy it would take to funnel it into her bank accounts. She'd dated Rod because they had fun together—in and out of the sheets.

The second reason was the same reason why Dedra had broken off her relationship with Big Daddy Rod: because he was a gambling addict.

When it became clear that he was ready to flush everything away, Dedra walked. She had more to think about than herself. Because, unlike Big Daddy Rod, Dedra loved her kid and was invested in keeping a future and legacy for her.

She could have felt bad for Creed, because, in the

end, his father had an addiction, and it tore the two apart and left Creed with nothing.

But he'd chosen this route, and seeing how he refused to let her get a word in and certainly wasn't about to see the truth, Dedra stamped out any sympathy she might have had. He didn't want to listen to why he was mistaken, so Dedra needed to choose: would she kill the little fucker with her bare human hands or shift into her super-sized goose to beat the shit out of him?

Ever seen a regular-sized Canadian goose go after someone? It was fucking scary.

Double the size of that goose? *Hahahah*, one couldn't even describe the terror.

Finally, she stood.

"What are you doing? Sit. *Down!*"

She made a big show of yawning and stretching, having easily snapped the zip ties off her wrists. "Look, baby boy. I'm about done here. Your daddy wasted your inheritance in casinos and racetracks around the world. Go look into his financial records, or ask any of his friends. Also, did you even look into me?"

"Yeah, you're loaded. With *my* money!" In a dumb move, he used the gun to tap his chest in emphasis. Dedra figured this kid had never handled a gun

before, which would make him even more dangerous. She needed to make this quick.

"No, little shit. With *my* money." She hissed the
words as her eyes narrowed. She knew the anger had
darkened her irises, based on the way Creed shriv-
eled back. It was enough to give her the opportunity
to snatch the revolver right from his limp hand. "I'm
from one of Canada's oldest mob families, and while
we might not be in power anymore"—due to the fact
that she was the last one, not counting her brother,
who'd been disowned—"you better bet that I've been
raised with enough of the Goosby fortitude to eat
your fucking head for breakfast and make sure no
one ever sees a fucking trace of your bloodline."

This time he definitely gulped. "I thought your
last name was Wakins."

"That was my husband's name, you fucking turd-
monger. Do some goddamn research before you go
off half-cocked next time." She popped the cylinder
out with care, not like that snap of the wrist they did
in the movies; she knew revolvers. She tilted it back
to empty the rounds into her hand, feeling their
weight and the cool touch of the brass in her palm.

She pushed the cylinder back into place and then
hurled the weapon into the water, since she couldn't
carry it in her goose form. Then, one by one, she

took the bullets and tossed them in after it, as if they were skipping stones.

Their dense, odd shapes didn't skip, but they made a satisfying *plunk* and little splash every time they hit the water.

"Will there b-be a next time for me... ma'am?" His fear was increased when a large fish jumped out of the water, attracted by the activity. Dedra couldn't tell, but it sure looked like the thing's pointed, gleaming teeth held one of the bullets in them.

Playing with him, she let her face soften, her eyes returning to their usual grey. When she wanted to, she could look motherly. Even though her touch on his cheek was gentle, he winced. "Oh, Creed, darlin', you didn't do anything wrong, right? You didn't hurt me. In fact, this little cruise has been enjoyable, if I can forget all the wretched bellyaching."

Even so, she wanted to make sure the little fucker didn't come around again. She moved her hand from his cheek to grab his chin in a vise-like grip. "But *please* don't fucking test me again. I do *not* do second chances."

And because she was absolutely sure that no one would ever believe him if he tried to talk about it, she shifted. She didn't strip first—he didn't get rewarded for his bumbling kidnapping attempt by getting to see her glorious body—which meant she tore out of her bikini and cover-up. Her human body transformed into the magnificent, giant grey and white Canadian goose.

She did it with her human arms out, which meant her goose appeared with wings spread wide. She kept her eyes on Creed the whole time, watching and reveling in the horror on his face. She let him take it all in for just a moment before she let out a deafening honk and then snapped at his face.

He screamed and crumpled to the floor of the boat. She was pretty sure he was shaking and crying, but she didn't need verification. She was done with him.

So she took flight.

2

Ever heard an ocelot laugh?

How about a crackle's cry?

An electric toothbrush?

It was all about the same noise, and it was the sound Andrés made when he watched Dedra Wakins read a garbage punk for filth.

Anyone looking in from the outside would be a bit confused to see a four-legged spotted cat curled up in a tree, cackling something fierce. Lucky for him, there were no people around.

Not so lucky was the fact that his hysterics almost cost him his mission. He was so caught up in his laughter that he wasn't ready when Dedra took off into the sky.

On the one hand, he could let her go. She'd likely just return to her hotel.

On the other hand, if Andrés was able to track her there, then so could the group who was out to get her. It would be better to grab her now, save a little trouble later.

Quickly, he made a calculation then ran for it, jumping along the best branches and then grabbing just the perfect one. He clung to the end of it, letting it sink lower and lower till just the right moment. He let go, dropping to the branch just below, and then watched the magic happen.

Ptew!

Gotcha!

It shot straight up, nailing his target.

And my mother said all those hours of playing Duck Hunt *on Nintendo were useless!*

Dedra squawked when the branch made impact, and he held his breath as she tumbled, realizing that if he miscalculated, then he might have actually hurt her.

He worried for nothing, though, because the goose landed on the next tree over, feathers ruffled but otherwise in one piece. As soon as her fall was stopped, she got to her webbed feet and spun around, mad as hell and looking for someone to blame.

She didn't have to look far. Her beady eyes locked on him, and she emitted a hiss that Andrés swore echoed through the jungle.

I ain't scared of no big chicken.

That was what he told himself, anyway, as he settled down on his branch, legs and paws tucked under him. It was a pose that was deceiving. He looked comfortable, but really he was coiling his body like a spring, ready to react if necessary.

The goose made her way down her branch, getting nearer to the neighboring tree. He watched it bow down with her great weight and kind of hoped that it would give way and stop this inevitable showdown.

A smaller bird, which had been making its home in one of the offshoots, flew up, chirping madly at Dedra for disrupting its nest.

In response, Dedra shot a wing out, colliding with it and rocketing the pretty blue-winged creature far behind her.

Gulp.

Sure, he could transform into his human shape, but where was the fun in that? That was for sure why he didn't change... it definitely had nothing to do with the fact that he didn't want his twig and berries anywhere near a snapping, snarling garburator—that was a garbage disposal, for all the non-Canadians—with wings.

Instead, he tried a different pose, sitting up on his hind ocelot legs, holding his paws down to the side. He liked to call this his meerkat pose. It was outrageously cute. Especially when he widened his eyes. Worked every time.

Well, almost every time. At that moment, it didn't seem to impress the goose. She took another step toward him, her branch bowing even more as her mouth pincer grew ever closer.

Andrés lifted one paw up in the air. *I come in peace.* She couldn't hear his thoughts, but he hoped she'd get the message.

Nope. Another step, this time lowering her neck and extending it in front of her. A clear sign that she was ready to fight.

For his next trick, he put both paws over his eyes and then quickly pulled them off—*boo!*—revealing a wide toothy cat grin. Surely that would help her see that he wasn't her enemy!

Still nope. Another step. He was sure that the branch was going to give out and drop out beneath her at any moment.

She must have been thinking the same thing, because she flapped her wings and made the jump to his branch, landing heavily and making him bounce.

He jumped, but not out of fear, definitely not!

Andrés had to work to keep from falling as the branch bobbed and swayed, threatening to catapult him off into kingdom come. He dug his claws into the wood, trying to stabilizing himself.

Before he could get himself back into some sort of dignified state, Dedra honked at him, lunging with her wings out. Andrés did his best not to flinch. He'd never admit it to the other agents, not in a million years, but it took everything in him to not shield his face with his little kitty arms.

Canadian Geese are fucking horrifying, okay?

He could take one out if he needed to, but he would like to avoid hurting Dedra, if at all possible. He hated having to fill out Target Accidental Injury Notification and Testimonies. TAINT forms blew the big one.

When he didn't react, Dedra halted and regarded him, cocking her head, on its long neck, to the side. He figured she must be wondering why this wild creature wasn't running in fear of the terrifying turkey.

Of course I'm not, bird brain! I'm a shifter, like you!

Joking time was over. He shifted into his human form, hooking one arm around the branch to keep from falling and using the other hand to cover his most valuable assets. "Hey now, lady, let's not try to kill a fellow!"

Not for the first time in her life, Dedra wished there was an easier way to identify a sentient animal. A shifter, that was.

You know, like a secret handshake or something. It would have been so helpful, growing up, to be able to meet others like herself in the wild.

That kind of technology did exist. Her family was stringent about using it when the family factory used real goose down. They ensured their down providers were certified dealers who used the tech so they knew they were never accidentally using shifters in their pillows and duvets.

They never made a version of it that was good for on-the-go, though. Like a laser scanner you could keep on you while you were shifted so you could scan a cat when it was acting like a weirdo. Green for shifter, red for real predator.

She watched the ocelot turn into a man—a damn

sexy one, if she were to take a moment to appreciate what was before her eyes—and once she saw that he wasn't about to lash out at her, she followed his lead.

She shifted, balancing with ease thanks to certain bird talents that translated to her human form. She allowed him to take a good look before saying, "Why the hell did you hit me?" It had really smarted, to get whacked by a branch mid-flight. The only explanation she could see was that the cat was responsible. She didn't often go looking to get into a scrap with another creature, sentient or not, but if it had wanted to start something, she'd deliver. Normally she'd stay away from lions and tigers, but she was sure she could take on a kitten like that.

Okay, ocelots weren't tiny or kittenish. She was well aware of how damn ferocious they could be. They fought with disregard for their own safety and could take down animals four times their size. They were the definition of savage.

But the kitty hadn't gone into any kind of offensive pose when she turned to face him. It was one thing for him to not run—sure, she could reason that an ocelot would be too tenacious to flee when something like her landed almost on its nose—but anything with an ounce of self-preservation would have at least prepared for a fight.

Unless it wasn't a normal wild ocelot.

Which, as it turned out, was the case. Unless Dedra was dreaming… because the tanned, handsome, tall drink of a man who now crouched in place of the ocelot was something that the best mail-order catalog of her dreams couldn't deliver.

He waggled his eyebrows, even though she thought his struggle to regain his composure was more comical and less sexy. "Welcome to my jungle," he said in a Brazilian accent that delighted her ears. He'd finally found his footing and stood on the branch, showing that his feline talents, at least for balancing, also translated to human form.

"Your jungle?" She looked around, surveying the dense foliage, and the animals you could pick out if you looked hard enough. "Does the wildlife here call you king, Tarzan?"

He made a face. "Tarzan is from Africa, *xuxu*."

She ignored the fact that in saying xuxu—which sounded like "chuchu"—he more or less had just called her *sexy lady*. She'd spent enough winters in the south to know a fair amount of Portuguese, but she didn't need to tell him that. "It's Dedra. And if you're not Tarzan, mind telling me who you are?"

He tossed his head, allowing the sun to sparkle in

his black hair and gleam off his toothy grin. "Andrés Sosa, FUC, at your service."

Dedra blinked. "Come again? Fuck at my service?" Had someone really ordered her a mail-order jungle gigolo? Hot damn!

The man started laughing. So much so that he hugged onto the tree trunk to steady himself while gasping for air. "FUC - eff you cee!! The Furry United Coalition, *xuxu*!" He dissolved into laughter again.

"Oh." Okay, that made more sense. Dedra knew all about FUC. Her family always did their best to stay out of their way. Taking on the shifter underworld was one thing, but having trained super agents on your tail was completely another. "What are you doing here? Are you here on vacation?" Or had she finally made a misstep big enough to draw the attention of FUC?

"You're in danger," he said. His laughter stopped, and his face turned serious.

He said danger. Not trouble. That was good, right? "What do you mean?" She thought about Creed, down there in his boat. He wasn't enough of a threat to send FUC to save her. That little dweeb probably couldn't successfully kill a spider.

"An unhinged group of animal activists is

protesting your company." He nodded solemnly, as though delivering life-altering news.

She waited for him to add to it. When he didn't, she added, "So? What else is new?" It happened all the time. They'd dealt in goose down for generations. Having animal activists protesting was *normal.* The only odd part about it was that this past year, after her father died, she had stopped using real down and changed everything to artificial fluff, so they technically weren't even in the down business anymore.

He seemed to have expected a different reaction from her. His mouth turned down. "This is serious. They're claiming to be a sect of MUFF, the Merrily United Furry Friends against the unethical treatment of non-sentient animals by shifters."

Hmmm, interesting. MUFF only went after shifters, and the fact that her family was shifters was a closely guarded secret. Hence the mob ties. It had always ensured that no one went digging into the Goosby family secrets.

So what would draw MUFF to them now? "Are you sure? How do you know this?" A ribbon of unease began to unfurl inside Dedra. Why hadn't she heard about this from her people at the factory? And how big was the trouble if FUC was involved?

"FUC has a long history with MUFF. We've disturbed the hornet's nest enough times that they like to taunt us whenever they're up to something. We received an official MUFF DIVE, Disclosure of Intent against Vile Enemies, just yesterday, and it identified you, and your company, as the target."

"Shit." That wasn't good. That meant MUFF knew she was a shifter.

More importantly, it meant that they might identify Kailee, her daughter, as well. And Dedra had no way to damage control that.

Luckily, FUC did. That was one of the things they specialized in.

"The good news is that now you have FUC on your side. We've tracked all of your family down—"

"Including Kailee?" She cut him off, not meaning to shoot dangerous daggers from her eyes at him. She couldn't help her protective mama-goose instincts.

"Yes, Kailee, Grayson, and Maddox"—her brother and nephew—"but before you fly off the handle, er, branch here, can you listen? FUC is on it, and we're bringing all four of you to our safe house."

"Kailee is in your custody?" Dedra's heart fluttered in her chest, panic threatening to cut in on this civil conversation and make her shift and fly north right then.

"I expect she is." Andrés was dusting himself off, looking like he was preparing to shift. "So, if you'll follow me, we can fly back to Canada together and you can see for yourself."

She'd rather just go herself, but she knew her wings were clipped. She had no recourse to protect her family from exposure by MUFF, and she knew FUC's reputation well enough to know that if they had Kailee in a safe house somewhere, then she couldn't be any better protected. Not only that, but she wouldn't be able to get near her daughter without a FUC agent escort.

So she agreed to go willingly with Andrés, back to Canada. "How the hell are you going to fly? You some fantasy hybrid cat that sprouts wings or something?"

"No, duckie," he said, giving her a wink that was so charming she *almost* didn't take offense at being called a duck. "This cat is a pilot."

3

Andrés reminded himself that a good FUC agent was trained for professionalism.

That meant not getting a boner when seeing a sexy naked lady.

But he couldn't help it. Nature was nature, you know? And he figured one could take it as an insult if there was a lack of bodily reaction. His boner was a compliment, so long as he didn't refer to it or try to use it without permission, right? If he didn't have wood, wouldn't she wonder, why not?

None of that mattered, though. Dedra's gaze never dipped low, or he at least didn't catch it doing so. Her loss—so he figured—but in return, he did his damndest to keep his eyes above the collarbone...

Her sexy, kissable, lickable, biteable collarbone...

He was glad she'd so readily agreed to leave with him. He needed a reason to stop being tempted to look at and appreciate her damn fine body.

He shifted back into his ocelot form and waited for her to shift into her goose form before he led her to his plane. The clumsy bird followed him through the jungle, taking to the air whenever she could, and being plenty vocal about how she felt about the abundance of branches in her way.

He was sure the goose was quite graceful when in open skies or on a nice lake, but damn if she didn't make a lot of honking noises behind him while being swatted by limbs or pelted by jungle bugs. They were treated to disgruntled sounds as they passed other birds, small primates, and reptiles who were none too pleased to be disturbed by the goose.

When they came upon his plane, he shifted back into human form, and she followed, jumping right in to give him an earful. "Were you *trying* to take the most complicated, crowded, chafing path? Because if so"—she started to golf clap, a slow and annoying noise—"then good job, Tarzan, you did it."

"It's Andrés, duckie, in case you forgot," he said, ignoring her other comments and punching in the digital key to unlock his plane while trying not to get another eyeful of her delicious body.

He did manage to catch the daggers she shot out of her eyes at him. "Okay, how about I won't say Tarzan again if you don't say duckie again. Because, so far, I've been one of the only Goosbys without a kill count, but if you say that word again, my leaderboard is going to change."

He laughed but agreed. "Okay, fair enough. I'm guessing turkey is also off the table?"

This time she took a swing at him, but he danced out of her reach. "Cat-like reflexes—"

"Say turkey again, I fucking dare you."

She was playing, right? Andrés wasn't entirely sure, based on the deadly look in her eyes, and he decided he better not continue to test her. He really didn't want to go back to his superiors and have to explain that he'd failed his mission because his flirting irritated the target into flying away without him.

"Truce, okay, I'm sorry, truce… okay?" Despite the apology, her face didn't soften. "I'm sorry, Dedra, you marvelous Canadian goose, the most majestic one I've ever been blessed to set eyes on." *In both human and goose form.*

That did the trick. The murder faded from her eyes, and he swore she preened at the compliment. It was too much for him; he had to turn away. The lady looked damn sexy when she basked in compliments like that. He could just imagine her in his bed while he worshiped her with his tongue—verbally and orally.

"I need your satellite phone." She interrupted his dirty thoughts. "I need to call Kailee."

He also needed to check in with his team, but he had a feeling that it was more important to let mother goose use the phone first, so he handed it over. He used the time while she was talking to get dressed and found it especially amusing when he heard Dedra ask her daughter, "Is your agent a hottie too?"

So she thinks I'm a hottie. Of course she did. All the ladies did. Men too. They couldn't resist the tan skin, the dimple, the elegant black coif that was starting to become salted in the most distinguished way. But the confirmation that Dedra thought of him that way seemed extra important to him. Was it because she was the first woman in a long time that he found not only very attractive but also interesting?

He'd have to save those thoughts for later. Once she was delivered to the FUC academy, his official mission was over. Till then, he'd keep it all in his pants.

After that… a cat could hope.

When she finished her phone call, he tossed her a FUC agent field package. "I brought you clothes."

"What the hell is this?" Her face scowled as she looked at the grey cotton shorts and matching grey tank top.

"The emergency clothes we keep for shifters in need of a quick cover."

"Granny panties?" She pulled them out from between the other clothes and held them up pinched between fingers.

He shrugged, trying to look serious, even though her offense to the items highly amused him. "It's the FUC-issued hot weather clothing kit. I didn't pick any of it."

"Well, you need to tell me who did, because I'm going to have a talk with them." He caught the wad of panty material she threw at him and didn't look up till he was certain she was dressed. How could someone look so sexy in such a simple set?

"You sure you don't want these? It will be a long flight?" he asked, squeezing the panties in his hand while trying not to think about the feel of the material on her velvety nether region.

"I'm good," she said while leaning into some downward-facing yoga pose.

Again, he had to look away. *Shit. The goose is going commando.*

That would make for quite an interesting distraction over the upcoming hours. How easy it could be to put on some autopilot and reach over to her lap...

"Can I see what info you have about MUFF and why they're targeting my family?" Once again, she pulled him out of his dirty thoughts. "I want to learn what I can about this weirdo cult."

He pulled out a tablet and tapped around on it before turning it over to her. She looked over the file as he warmed up the plane engines and called into the office. Alyce, his boss and the academy director, answered right away.

"Just checking in, target acquired, and we're on schedule to make it to our stopover safe house tonight."

The safe house was already booked for him. Even with the extra FUC tech that made his plane go faster and farther on less gas, they would still need to make a few fuel stops and would definitely need to stop for the night. Andrés could fly for only so many hours before he needed to take a break. Despite the advances of FUC technology, they still hadn't come up with a way to make people not need any sleep, and Andrés didn't play with safety by flying while tired.

"Good work, Sosa. Any problems?"

"It's been pretty smooth sailing." The Creed boy wasn't worth mentioning; neither was their flirty banter. His boss just wanted to know if there was any movement from MUFF.

"Great. Our contacts in air traffic control will make sure to track you and to clear you through borders. Have a safe flight."

He'd barely ended the call when Dedra asked him, "Where are we landing tonight?"

"That's need-to-know information," he told her, opening the passenger door for her to hop in.

"And I need to know." She didn't budge.

"For what?" he asked. "It's a safe house. People aren't to know you're there."

"Because I'm not wearing this for two days and overnight. If you don't want me to disclose the safe house location, then let me know where one of the fuel points will be. They'll drop my package there."

"Postmates isn't going to just wait around for you. You'll just have to deal."

"Postmates?" She laughed. "Oh, honey, we don't use anything that mundane. I'm a NAKED girl."

The statement conjured an image of Dedra nude.

He didn't even need to use his imagination. The picture was perfectly clear in his mind, no matter how hard—*exactly, hard because I didn't try at all*—he'd tried to not look at her.

"Hey." She clapped her hands, bringing him back to their clothed reality. "NAKED is the Network for Apparel and Kit Express Delivery. It's the way we geese can fly across the country and not get caught in our birthday suits. We set up an order, indicate a drop point, and it's hidden there waiting for us when we arrive."

It made sense, and even though he'd much rather have her in the tiny pieces of fabric for two days, he relented and gave her the satellite phone and their first US-based fueling location.

Dedra wasn't happy to be heading back to Canada so early in the season. This was her time for sunshine. She never forced herself to be around a cold winter if she could help it.

She kept her mind occupied with thoughts of the weather because, otherwise, she didn't like how dark her thoughts could go. It was one thing to mess with the factory. She'd been raised a businessperson and was ready to take on whatever trouble happened, but her father hadn't prepared her for what it would feel like to have a kid in danger.

Had he felt like this when she was being held by strangers, bingeing on chocolate and regaling strangers with her Little Orphan Annie songs?

She had to sit tight and just not think about it. She couldn't do anything about it. She'd talked to Kailee, heard her voice, been assured she was fine and was in good hands. They were both on their way to the safe house and would be together soon. Now Dedra just had to think about other things.

There was one easy thing she could focus on… like how sexy Andrés looked when examining the lights on his console or tapping stuff into his tablet. She'd mentioned the mile high club, but so far, he'd acted disinterested. He'd told her that he was a good pilot and flying them safely was the only job he was doing while in the air.

Really! A job? *The nerve!*

The responsible-aviator routine only made her hotter for him.

At least Andrés' Cessna was beautiful on the inside, full leather and luxury. It had extra bells and whistles, so he told her, which meant that they'd make it in half the time with fewer stops to refuel. It meant that at least she could be comfortable physically, even if, inside, she was trying to bury a stampede of fears.

And at their first US stop, Dedra collected her NAKED order. She didn't care if Andrés would call her a diva for getting so much stuff. She had the resources, so why not use them? She needed clothing, toiletries, makeup, not to mention a new phone and a few good romance novels to make the ride go by faster. She'd even ordered a pretty little passport wallet for the identification FUC had provided.

Even with the big haul, she didn't bother changing yet. She wanted to shower before she put on her new stuff, and she didn't want to take the extra time at their first stop. She could wait till they got to the overnight safe house.

Plus, she kind of liked hanging out in the skimpy shorts and tank. Even if he was playing hard to get, she still caught the way his eyes got stuck to certain areas on her body.

As she pulled the large suitcase, makeup case, and purse to the plane, she heard him call over to her. "That was all hiding for you somewhere here?"

She shrugged. "Yep."

"We're in a tiny Cessna! You can't have all that!"

She rolled her eyes. "Sure I can. Your plane

would seat five, and there's just two of us. You're lucky I didn't ask for them to put a puppy in here too."

He made a face.

"Ah, right, you're a cat person. Well, dogs are more fun to travel with."

"I take offense to that!"

Oh, how much she was tempted to move in close to his offended body and make up for it with a kiss... She wondered if he thought the same. Not that he'd tell her, being Mr. Business and all, but she had a feeling that the two of them might be some kind of magic if given a chance.

Andrés was like no man she'd dated before, yet he was just her type. He wasn't just a stuffy rich guy who wanted to pay top dollar for concierge. Andrés was adventurous, sexy, bold, daring, did she mention sexy? She'd never had a man fly her—in his own aircraft!—for their travels. Andrés was the kind of guy that she could have only hoped would walk across her luxury resort view.

If only they weren't heading back to Canada.

Maybe she could convince him to fly them back to Brazil once MUFF was taken care of.

And at least she could enjoy one last night of warmth since their safe house stop was in California. One final night before returning to Canada's icy embrace.

The safe house was at a FUC private airstrip. They went directly there after landing. Dedra was ready to stretch her legs by that point but also ready to wash off the cabin air.

"Do you want to shower?" she asked Andrés, knowing his answer but still hoping he'd give in.

"You can go first." He was hauling in her luggage and barely sparing her a glance.

"California has a water crisis. We can do our part for the environment by showering together." She dropped her eyes and smiled at him.

"*Xuxu*, make no mistake, I care about the environment, but the two of us in the shower"—he walked over to her and brushed a strand of hair from her face—"will not be water-saving. It will be long and hot." He trailed his hand down her neck and hovered at her collarbone before he abruptly turned away.

She caught her breath. "Well, then you go first. I don't like sitting around, ready to go but having to wait on the other person."

He looked back at her, shrugged, but said nothing as he grabbed his bag and went to the bathroom.

Dedra took her time to examine the room they

were staying in. It had a separate living room, kitchen, bedroom, and bathroom area but was decorated as simply as an ordinary hotel room. It didn't seem to be fancy at all, but Andrés had told her that it was bomb-proof and completely off all radar. That, plus it was clean. That was the important part. Whoever maintained it had made sure they had clean sheets and coffee, which was all anyone really needed from a stopover point.

She was flipping through the TV channels when Andrés emerged from the bathroom. She'd hoped she'd be able to see him half-naked and wet, with just a towel around his waist, and she wasn't disappointed. What she wasn't prepared for was her body's reaction to the scent of him. He was now clean of all the airplane and jungle smells, and the mixture of body wash, deodorant, aftershave, pheromones, whatever, was just a glorious cocktail of sexy man that made Dedra want to throw him down on the queen-sized bed and take him all in, head to toe.

But he barely spared her a glance as he dressed. "It's all yours. I'm going to check in with FUC and go over the post-flight plane check. Don't open the door to anyone while I'm gone."

So, he wanted to play it like that. Sure, he was on

a mission and shouldn't fuck his target. Fine by her. Waiting made it even better in the end.

And the game alone was fun.

Good thing she'd gone all out with her NAKED order. She had everything she needed to return her look to the Dedra Wakins standard. That included purple shampoo to brighten her platinum hair, her favorite makeup brands, the right bra to show off the twins, tight leather pants that she knew screamed "do me," and an irresistible perfume that she only used for the most deserving men.

She finished her look with a beige lace top with a plunging neckline and a long diamond pendant necklace to give her just a bit of extra sparkle. It was a sexy look, no doubt, but still elegant and dignified.

The NAKED folks were used to extravagant orders from rich clients. She tipped them well when they did a job well done. And in this case, it was especially well done, based on the way Andrés ogled her when he came back and caught sight of her.

She basked in his look of astonishment, trying not to look too smug. *You like what you see, kitty?* It was ironic that she felt like the cat who ate the canary, when really she was the fowl and he was the feline.

"You were in there forever," he said.

She didn't let her smile falter. She knew he just didn't want to admit he appreciated the view. She'd noticed the movement in his pants. He was just a few beats away from looking up and howling "ah-oo-gah!"

"I clean up nice, don't I, Andrés?" She purred his name.

His gulp was visible. "I'm impressed. You did a lot in a small amount of time with just my phone."

"I can do more with less when I need to." She took a step toward him.

"Yeah, but you looked tasty in the gray stuff too." He touched her arm, sending a shiver through her body.

"Honey, I molted those like last year's down. I can only tolerate low-grade cotton-polyester mixes for so long." She pressed close to him and felt his erection on her hip. "But I appreciate that you had me covered. You should let me repay you."

She tilted her chin and fluttered her eyes closed, willing him to break and kiss her.

He didn't.

She felt his hands on her shoulders as he stepped back from her.

Damn it. She wouldn't show her disappointment

though. "Where are we going for dinner?" she asked sweetly, changing the subject.

"We'll hop in a car and go down to a local seafood joint. You like seafood, right?"

"Of course." She walked by him, going for the door, letting him get a good view of her swaying backside. She glanced over her shoulder to make sure he was looking. "Coming?"

4

Jimmy and his co-workers at the Goosby Bedding factory had a plan, and everything was falling into place.

Since Mr. Goosby had passed, his shrew of a daughter had changed everything at the factory. The workers' frustration had been growing, and Jimmy finally took it upon himself to organize the dissenters, those who wanted to stand up against her.

His group didn't like the loss of values. The factory was a cultural institution that used to stand for something real and meaningful. Now they had new fancy machines that did more work than the people had to, and even the pillow stuffing was artificial.

The writing was on the wall. Dedra was setting the factory up to run itself, with very little manpower. Soon there would be no need for more than half the staff. Just because she said now that they were all going to keep their jobs didn't make it true. Hell, he was pretty sure she'd sell it all off, shut it all down, whatever. Anyone who could change from real down to fake was as imitation as they came.

She couldn't be trusted.

Jimmy's group had been able to stir up some of the public, but it wasn't enough. Some folks got fired up and took to social media, but it didn't get much traction. It seemed most people were in support of the changes Dedra implemented, which infuriated Jimmy. He was starting to think he was out of ammunition.

Then the package arrived.

It was a USB drive that had one file. A video.

At first, Jimmy didn't know what in the hell he was looking at. It seemed to be some kind of shaky home movie, filmed vertically on a cell phone. Dedra was in the middle of a field. You could see her face clearly, although she wasn't looking at the camera; she seemed to be looking at someone near it. Then she took a few steps away, shedding her clothes, and then she disappeared. In the spot where she was, a large Canadian goose took off into the air.

The last thing on the video was a black screen with a phone number and the word *MUFF*.

He replayed the whole thing over and over, trying to figure out the trick he was watching, and then he finally gave up and Googled the phone number and MUFF.

He learned that MUFF stood for "Merrily United Furry Friends against the unethical treatment of non-sentient animals by shifters." Their shady website told tales of people who could turn into animals, who called themselves "shifters." MUFF stood against them and stood up for the normal animals that were harmed by them.

Jimmy let all of this percolate in his mind for a bit before he decided to take the leap. They needed something that could get them international attention, and that was what this group seemed like it could do. If MUFF came to Goosby and supported their cause, Jimmy and his team would be able to out Dedra, turn the factory back to the old ways, and have things back to the old ways.

But he knew he had to make the pitch in a certain

way, in order to get MUFF to agree to help them. In his first call to them, he explained the video and told them what Dedra had done. "If we don't do something, she's going to cause the extinction of all the geese! No one will want them anymore! It's not like we can put them in a zoo or something!"

The cultists fell for it.

And they moved fast. Before Jimmy knew it, they'd set a day to meet on-site at the factory. He hadn't been sure that they would buy into the whole "think of the geese!" plea, but Lady Luck brought him one more surprise to help him along.

A goose, live and in the flesh, er, down.

"Oh mighty Lenny, please, in your wisdom, tell us how we must act next." He put on a show as he walked through the factory floor behind the thing. He'd found Lenny wandering outside the factory and learned his name thanks to the tattoo on one of the goose's webbed feet. It seemed trained, even responded to words, and Jimmy immediately realized that this was the perfect mascot. Having the thing around was just what they needed to make sure MUFF would help them.

MUFF wouldn't know that Jimmy was full of shit, that he didn't believe this goose was anything special, but it would serve a purpose. He'd got his co-dissenters to agree to the faux-worship of Lenny, and they'd been making big shows of lavishing praise on the bird.

Now for the big show. Jimmy was on his way to meet the MUFF members, walking with Lenny by the non-dissenting employees, past the machine that blew and combed the unnatural fluff, past the rollers that made webs that would be folded into the pillows and duvets. He looked at the clueless lemmings, his coworkers who acted like they were so happy to have updated machinery. Didn't they know that those machines were going to replace them all eventually? That they were at the end of days if they didn't act now?

The goose marched through the workshop, and some workers did a double-take. They weren't used to seeing a live goose in their midst. A bit of fluff puffed off of a conveyor belt, floating to the ground in front of Lenny. The goose turned up his beak at it.

"How dare you insult Lenny by throwing fluff at him!" Jimmy yelled.

"Shut up, Jimmy," the worker said. "Get that thing out of here before I decide to pluck him and make my own pillow."

Lenny squawked at that and flapped his wings, picking up speed as he made his way to the floor overseer's office, where they'd been keeping and feeding him.

It was also where the MUFF representatives were waiting for them. This meeting was important. Even though MUFF had already agreed to help them, they'd made it clear that they could back out at any time. Jimmy knew it was a hard sell, getting them to support the idea that getting rid of natural down was risking the extinction of the goose species and that it was decreasing their value on this earth.

Jimmy walked into the office after he opened the door for Lenny. Jimmy's lackeys, Seamus and Pearlene, had met the MUFF members outside and brought them in, where they were all waiting to meet Jimmy and Lenny.

"So glad you all could come and support us in this endeavor." Jimmy, Seamus, and Pearlene met MUFF members Vergie, Elon, and Brain. And of course, they introduced Lenny.

Jimmy already had an idea that these folks would be creepy, based on their weird website, but he thought the black robes and hoods over their head with the gold embroidery was a bit over the top.

Even so, the factory rebellion needed them if they were to be heard.

The leader, Brain, got down on one knee. "Hello, Lenny," he said with reverence. "Thank you for taking on this mission, for doing the work of the geese who have been silenced."

Lenny, in true goose fashion, screamed and pecked at the cultist, getting him right in the cheek, barely missing his eye.

Jimmy held his breath, certain the stupid bird had just ruined everything.

The cultist fell forward, holding himself up with his hands and knees, looking like he was bowing to Lenny. "You're right, Lenny. I will pay penance on behalf of the humans of the world who have betrayed your kind. If you choose to make an example of me, I will take it."

Jimmy let out his breath and looked over to Seamus and Pauline. Pauline whispered to him, "What kind of cock-a-doodle-doodle is this guy running on?"

"Who the hell cares? If we want this factory to get back to the old ways, then we need them to help us go viral or whatever. To get more folks behind us. Whatever it takes."

Brain finally stood and turned to the three factory dissenters. "We will be glad to join your cause. We've already issued a MUFF DIVE to members of FUC to announce our intentions of action against Dedra Wakins. What would you like to see happen next?"

Jimmy smiled. "It's simple."

Before he could finish, Lenny squawked and flew up, attacking a wall. He targeted a framed photo, knocking it to the ground. The glass cracked, but they could still make out the photo of the Wakins family.

"We take out Dedra Wakins," Jimmy translated. "If we get rid of her, we can get the geese back."

They'd shared a good meal the night before, but Dedra remained sexually frustrated, as Andrés hadn't budged in his stance on no touching.

All in good time. Dedra had other ways to pass the hours, including texting with Kailee to get all the details of *her* adventure with her FUC agent. Between texts, she played a match-three game on her new phone and then ended the night finishing one of the hockey sports romance books she'd bought.

So, not all a complete loss.

But by the next day, the novelty had worn off, and Dedra was feeling stifled by the tiny aircraft and quite annoyed that her vacation had been ruined. She was ready to get down to business, to deal with MUFF, and return to sun tanning on the beach.

Instead of reading, since she'd finished all the books NAKED had dropped off, she passed the flight by asking questions.

"What do you do for FUC?" she asked Andrés.

"I'm currently a professor at the academy." His answer seemed purposely vague.

"What do you teach?" She wondered if he had some super-secret FUC reason to be cagey about it or if he were embarrassed to admit what it was.

"How about you tell me about you instead? I'm curious how you can run such a big company but still travel south for the winter." As they'd been coasting for a while at the same altitude, he was able to sit comfortably in his chair and look at her, only occasionally glancing at the tablet that gave him the readouts.

Damn, he looks sexy surrounded by all those controls.

"I have a lot of good people in place who run it in

my absence." He seemed to be playing it cool, so she did the same. She didn't want to throw herself at him and look desperate. She didn't need to be desperate. Just because Andrés seemed like he'd been dropped on her right from the heavens didn't mean she was going to act foolish for him.

"And there were no murmurs of an uprising before you left?" He leaned in his chair, his hand casually dropping off the armrest and brushing her arm, sending a jolt through her. Dedra stiffened but refused to respond further. She knew he was just playing with her.

"No. I made a lot of changes this past year, but I kept the workers informed the whole way. I promised them that nothing would happen to their jobs and even gave people a chance to leave with a generous package if they wanted to." It kind of annoyed her to think that some of them had plotted against her. She wanted to know who and why, but she didn't dare call in and ask anyone about it. She would check in with the FUC team at the academy and see what intel they had before she alerted anyone at the factory that she was wise to what was going on. Andrés said it was the best way to ensure that the workers and MUFF didn't decide on any drastic action right away.

"What kind of changes?" He seemed truly intrigued, and she liked it. Most men didn't care to hear about her business. She ran a finger over his hand, looking at his gorgeous fingers, wishing she could do more. His fingers responded to her touch, reaching out for her, caressing hers.

"There were certain things my brother never liked about the company. My father refused to change, and my brother walked away. I didn't, but I knew that when my father passed the company to me, I'd make the changes that would bring my brother back." Although they were on the topic of business, her body was elsewhere. How could playing with fingers be so sexy?

"He walked away? That must have infuriated your father." He closed her hand around hers, holding it still. She looked from their hands to his deep brown eyes.

"Yeah." It had. And it broke her heart when it happened. "Grayson came back around when his son, Maddox, was old enough to want to know his family, but Grayson and Dad were too stubborn to fully make amends. Dad died after Mom did and left everything to me. I wanted to make sure Grayson got half of it, but he refused to take it as long as it was 'blood money,' as he called it."

He squeezed her hand and then rubbed the top of it with his thumb. "So you got rid of real down and moved to fake fluff, and that's enough to bring him back?"

"I was hoping so. My dad always called him a bleeding heart. He hated geese getting killed. Really hated it. He'd scream if our parents tried to get him to go to the factory, even though we didn't kill geese there; we just had the down delivered. He threw down pillows and duvets out of his bedroom window if they tried to give them to him. He walked away and never wanted any part of it."

"You two are still close, though. How do you leave for so long without any way to talk to him or your kids or even anyone at the factory? You don't check in with them for the whole winter?"

"Wrong." Dedra shook her head. "I fly a specific path, so they know where I should be, and when. I stay in hotels, having a pre-arranged package from NAKED ready for me at each stop with clothes and a throwaway phone. I check in at certain times. Otherwise, my workers and kids won't know I haven't been hit by a plane or some shit." It happened. More often than she liked to think about. Sometimes shifters were bigger than the average non-sentient animal, but humans couldn't tell the difference. And if you zoned out while coasting through the clouds, planes could sneak up on you.

"So, they know where you're staying when you get to your end spot."

"Bingo." She pulled her hand from him, wanting to shake off the intimacy she was feeling, and tapped her temple. "This isn't new. My people have been doing this forever. Now that we have the internet, it's easier to coordinate." It also helped that she had plenty of money to pay NAKED from wherever she was.

As if reading her mind, he commented, "And your family fortune probably also helps." She'd seen that look before. He wasn't asking about a fortune made from pillows.

People either loved or hated the fact that her people were from a mob. "Sure," she said cautiously, knowing that, with his FUC intel, he likely knew plenty about her family's past, but she wasn't going to offer up details, any more than he was going to tell her about his FUC duties.

"I heard what you told that boy. About your family." His face was stony. She couldn't tell if he was being judgmental or merely curious.

She shrugged. "Rumors. Legend. Lore. Enough to keep little shitheads like him from trying to come at me again." But she gave him a little smile while she pulled out a tiny—airplane-appropriate sized, even if she wasn't flying commercial—bottle of gin and took a swig. It wasn't her usual martini, but it was better than nothing. Then she winked at him.

"A lady of secrets. I can respect that."

"And you? You're a pilot. And you can apparently figure out exactly what branch to use to knock a flying goose out of the jungle. What does that make you, some kind of engineer or mathematician?" She watched his face closely for any sign of a tell.

"Nope."

"Seriously? You're not going to tell me what you do? Is it something lame, like basket weaving?"

"I'll have you know basket weaving isn't lame." He raised an eyebrow and smiled. "It goes along with old skills like tying knots to make nets. It's historically a very important trade."

"Fine. Do they offer a basket weaving or net-making course at the academy?"

He shrugged and offered her a tight-lipped smile that she couldn't read. "I can't say one way or another."

"I've opened up to you. You gotta give me something." She meant it. She did want to get to know him. They'd spent this much time together already, and she didn't like feeling like it was all one-sided.

He surprised her by leaning toward her, close enough for his lips to touch her ear while he spoke his next words. "Take my word that I'll let you know what you need to know, and when I can, I'll tell you more."

5

Andrés waited until they were on the final leg of their journey to hit her with the secretive forms. There would be no turning back then.

"This is why you wouldn't talk to me about your job or anything FUC-related? Because I'd yet to sign this?" she asked, skimming the document on his tablet while he drove his truck, which they'd picked up at the private British Columbia airstrip.

Andrés nodded, keeping his mouth shut until she had time to read it all over and sign it. From this point forward, she was going to be privy to the secret world of FUC, and she had to agree to keep all knowledge quiet.

To the outside world, FUCN'A, the Furry United Coalition Newbie Academy, was ARSHOL, the

Animal Rescue Special House of Learning. They had tons of land up in the Rocky Mountains, with trees and lakes and rivers running through it. There was plenty of room for cadets to train in their human or animal forms. And if anyone managed to get through the communication blockers and get some footage of animals running around, they could explain it away as a part of the animal training center.

At the gate, Andrés greeted the security attendant. The guard looked over to Dedra and back to Andrés. "You got the TURDS?"

Andrés grimaced. Whoever named the Truthful and Unfettered Reconciliation to Defend our Secrets must have hated the agents. Why not just call it a non-disclosure agreement? Was it really worth it to call it a TURDS form instead of an NDA?

Dedra's snicker seemed to answer that question. Andrés shook his head and handed over the tablet. The guard looked it over then nodded, handing it back to him and then opening the gate. "Enjoy your stay, Ms. Wakins."

"You have a marvelous day!" she called out as Andrés was putting up the window and driving onto the academy grounds.

She excitedly watched out the window to get

peeks of the cadets. They were running drills, practicing the obstacle courses.

"I haven't known very many other shifters, you know," she told him.

"Really?" Andrés couldn't imagine a life like that. His parents had made sure he had a solid network of shifters to turn to when he was growing up. Especially when they'd moved from South America to Canada. They believed it was important to have a big support system.

"Yeah, only geese when I was growing up but, even then, not many. My family had secrets, and my father treated our shifting ability the same as he did some of his, well, *different* business ventures."

"What about Kailee's dad?" As soon as the question came out, Andrés felt weird about it. He was interested in Dedra, and asking about her deceased husband felt awkward.

"Meeting him was a fluke. We met in university. I guess something pulled our animals together. Let me tell you, though, was it ever hard to get around to admitting it to each other! The shifting part, that is. You start out kind of like, 'hey, wouldn't it be cool if people could turn into animals' and then start to feel it out from there." She laughed a little, seeming to look off in the distance while the memory floated in her head, and when he glanced at her, he saw some sadness in her face.

"He was a goose too?" Andrés asked, unable to figure out a good way to change the subject without seeming insensitive.

"Oh, no!" Dedra exclaimed, turning to him. "Not at all! He was a narwhal!"

Andrés swerved a little, causing the cadets on the grass to look at them. He waved, a gesture to tell them all was all right. "How in the hell did that work?"

"Well, he loved swims in cold water, but he'd jump on a plane and come south with me for vacation. I just stuck to shorter southern migrations when he was around. Kailee takes after him, you know."

"She's a narwhal?" As much as Andrés had grown up around shifters, he hadn't been around very many large marine mammals before. Otters, sure. But whales or narwhals, never.

"She is." He liked the pride he saw in her face as she talked about her daughter. "Early on, I'd been a little sad not to have a little gosling to keep under my wing, but the time she spent out there, swimming with her dad, are moments she'll treasure forever, so I'm glad she took after him."

Again, a sad moment. Andrés cleared his throat. "Were you able to raise Kailee around more shifters, compared to your youth?"

"I tried," Dedra explained. "But it's not like there's a secret handshake or something. I'm actually excited for her to be around the FUC people. It might help her find her place in the world." She pulled out her phone and started typing on it. Andrés figured all the talk about Kailee had prompted Dedra to send her a text.

They'd finally driven far enough in where they could see the main building. It was huge, but it had even more space underground. "Tell Kailee that there's a saltwater pool. Two, actually. One warm, one cold. They're enormous; she'll love it."

Dedra looked at him, her head cocked to the side, a small smile on her face. "Yeah, that does sound like something she'd like."

———

His one small comment about Kailee liking the swimming pools warmed Dedra's heart. She loved her daughter and wanted the best for her, and it was a special feeling to think that someone else was looking out for Kailee too.

Andrés let her know that the main building was the Working and Administration Networking Core—she could tell he was doing his best to not call it "WANC"—and he guided her to the front desk where they verified her ID and TURD form and gave her keys to a room in return.

"We'll have a cadet take your bags up for you, ma'am," the desk agent told her. "Right now, they'd like you both to head to the meeting."

Dedra didn't bother asking "what meeting." She automatically assumed it would be a meeting pertaining to her case. Why else would they want her there?

As Kailee had just texted that they were only now boarding the plane to BC from Japan, Dedra knew she wouldn't be there, but she was elated to see her brother, Grayson, and nephew, Maddox, when she walked into the room.

They both met her with a big group hug. "You guys! It's so good to see you!" It really was. She hadn't realized how much she needed them to be there. She'd been trying to be so relaxed and nonchalant about the danger, but now that she saw them in the flesh, she had to admit that she'd been worried.

"Where's Kailee?" Grayson asked, looking behind her.

"Oh, you know my little chickie. She's taking her sweet time, enjoying the trip from Japan back over here. I'm sure giving her agent a run for his money. I've been texting her, though, and she should be in tomorrow." More nonchalance, because she was determined to stay strong. She would worry until her baby—it didn't matter if she was twenty, she'd always be her baby—was in her arms, but she was going to keep the Goosby stiff upper lip until then.

Andrés introduced her to the other agents around the table, which included Viktor and Renee Smith, Mason Brownsmith, and Jessie Cygnclair—or at least, Dedra had known Jessie, the Canadian swan princess, as Cygnclair. She wasn't sure if she'd taken Mason's last name or not.

As soon as Dedra finished meeting everyone, Alyce Cooper, the FUCN'A director, entered the room. "Welcome to the academy, Dedra, Grayson, and Maddox. I'm sorry we're not meeting under better circumstances, but I'm happy to extend some hospitality and offer my academy as a safe house and local base of operations for our agents."

Dedra appreciated the stern, serious look on Alyce's face. She looked like she meant business.

Dedra also thought that she looked like the kind of woman who might be fun to hang out with, when she wasn't hyper-focused on a task at hand.

"Thank you all," Dedra said, "for taking this on, for helping our family."

"It's only because of MUFF's involvement," the ornery croc, Viktor, explained. "We keep trying to stomp them out, but they keep popping up all over the place."

Renee draped her arm around Viktor's shoulder. Dedra couldn't help but notice her beautiful long red hair. "What my husband meant to say is we're happy to be of service."

"What I don't understand is why they would come against us now. Our family has been in the goose-down business for generations, and just this past year, we stopped using animal feathers and switched to synthetic down. It's been in all our marketing. It was a major thing."

Mason chimed in. "Looks like someone from your factory contacted them, and they sprang at the chance to create chaos."

"If you're thinking this isn't adding up yet, then let me fill in the blanks." Jessie looked at Dedra with a level gaze that said she wasn't going to hide anything from her. "MUFF only takes action in situations where shifters are involved."

Dedra's heart stilled. "They can't know I'm a shifter."

Jessie nodded her head then pointed a remote at the projection screen. Images of emails popped up. "One of your employees got ahold of a video of you shifting and sent it to MUFF. I was able to track the communication, but I haven't yet been able to find the video or figure out who sent the email. Only that the IP address is from the factory."

Andrés squeezed Dedra's shoulder. "It's going to be okay."

"How?" She looked at him helplessly. "The Goosbys managed to keep the family secret for generations, and I'm in charge for one year and the goose is out!"

"It's not your fault," Alyce said, her voice stern. "We're all facing more challenges. Now that people have cell phones, videos pop up all over the place. Most of the time we can corrupt the files and erase the evidence—"

"Already done that!" Jessie chimed in. "MUFF might know you're a shifter, but they won't be able to tell anyone else."

"You're leaving out the fact that they may have made backups," Dedra said miserably.

"I have a script running to search for anything that might pop up with the same footprint as this video," Jessie said. When Dedra gave her a confused look, she added, "Think of it as a little internet buddy whose whole job is to hang out online and watch for this video. As soon as it sees any piece of the video, it will rip it to shreds."

Dedra managed a smile at the image. "I don't really know how all that works, but I'll trust you."

Dedra looked back to Alyce. "What do we do now?"

"Relax," Alyce said. "Go take a swim or enjoy the shooting range. We've got this handled. You can see we have some of our best agents here—"

"You mean *now* we do!" a loud, bouncing female voice called out from the doorway. "That's right, people. I'm here!"

6

"Oh my God, you're Miranda!" Dedra gushed, a sound Andrés hadn't expected could come out of her.

Miranda preened, cocking her head to the side and letting everyone take a moment to admire her buxom blond-bombshell physique. "The one and only! You didn't think I was going to miss out on the fun, did you?"

Andrés was glad to see Miranda. Not only was she the best-of-the-best when it came to FUC agents, but she was also the only person he knew who could cheer up anyone, no matter the situation. And Dedra needed that right now. Miranda's cheerfulness was infectious, and she was also the kind of kick-ass lady who would make sure no one lay around and moped.

While Dedra and Miranda talked, Andrés took a moment to speak to Alyce. "I'd like to stay on the case," he said, looking at the team of agents as he said it.

"Your part of the mission is complete. Job well done," Alyce said. "We've had quite a few students asking when you'd return. Apparently, they're not impressed with your temporary replacement."

Damn, he hoped it would be easier than this. "I just mean I've had some time to get to know Dedra, learn about her family, and I think it would be good if I could stick around, in case she needs anything."

"Oh." Renee let out a little gasp. "You *like* her."

He turned to argue with her but then decided there was no point. "Who can blame me?" he said finally. "Honestly, I'm not going to be much good to the students if my head is on this case instead of in the classroom with them."

"Sure, your head's on the case... not in the gutter," Mason commented, earning him an elbow from Jessie. "Ow! Okay, look, bro, it happens. I know from experience." He cocked a thumb over to his wife.

Alyce's eyes hadn't moved from Andrés' face, and

though the squint was almost imperceptible, Andrés knew she was analyzing him. While he was jokingly referred to as a ladies' man around campus, he never actually acted on anything like that. He was a flirt, but in the time he'd been there, he'd never actually been involved with anyone.

"Okay," Alyce said finally. She held up a hand before Andrés could thank her. "Thing is, I can't put you on the mission, because of this interest of yours. I'm authorizing you taking some leave so you can stick around, but in an unofficial capacity."

Score. It was better than being on the case because that meant he was free and clear to pursue Dedra.

He heard Viktor chuckle. "Good luck, my man."

Andrés saw Viktor look over at Renee and saw the man's face soften. Andrés had the distinct feeling that while Viktor may have sounded like he was joking, he might have really meant it. Viktor had a reputation for being a hard-ass, but the way he was with Renee showed that even the most obstinate of them could melt with the right person.

Could Andrés have that with Dedra? There was only one way to find out.

Walking back over to Dedra and Miranda, he heard the bouncing bunny trying to ruin his plans for the night. "Let's go do something fun! Chase is on daddy duty, and I'm free as a bird!"

Andrés cleared his throat. "Um, aren't we supposed to keep the Goosby family in the facility?"

"Who said we were going to leave? I can make a party anywhere! Just give me some carrot cake and make her some martinis, and we'll be set! Hey, Alyce, you in?"

"I thought you were here to lead the team?" Mason shouted over to his sister-in-law. "Get over here and stop cockblocking."

Miranda gasped and spun to look at Andrés with wide eyes and then turned back to Dedra. "Girl! You did *not* tell me it was like that! I'll take a rain check. You go get yours!" She flew across the room to grab Andrés' hand and then shoved both of them out of the room.

The door slammed shut behind them.

Dedra was full of all sorts of different emotions.

She was relieved and happy to see her brother and nephew. She was anxious to see Kailee soon. She was annoyed with the factory workers and MUFF and nervous about the fact that her shifter secret had gotten out somehow. And she was thrilled to meet a legendary FUC agent, Miranda.

But none of that mattered. Grayson and Maddox had gone up to bed, saying they were tired from their trip. Kailee was on a plane and out of communication.

And now she was alone with Andrés.

He escorted her up to her room, which she'd figured would be some lousy dorm setup, but she was pleasantly surprised to see that it was a fully furnished VIP suite with all the amenities she could ask for at a five-star hotel.

"We have to be able to accommodate all sorts of people," Andrés explained as they walked inside.

"I get that, but I didn't know *I* ranked as an important person to FUC."

"You're important to me." He spoke in a low purr, leaning against a wall and waggling his eyebrows at her.

"That's cheesy as fuck," she told him, giving his shoulder a little shove. "You can do better."

"You'll have to forgive me. My best lines are buried underneath all of the thoughts of your naked body that have been floating around in my head for two days." He reached out to touch her neck and stroked down her collarbone, making her skin tingle.

"You could have told a girl, you know?" Dedra said, placing her hand on his chest and letting herself get lost in his eyes. "We didn't have to act, but not telling me how you felt was a bit unfair."

"When you walked out in that little lace top and tight leather pants, I almost lost it right there." He leaned down and spoke into her ear, again igniting sparks that flowed from top to bottom inside her. "It was all I could do not to have you in the room last night, or touch you at all in the plane. Talking about it wasn't going to do me any favors. I had to keep my mind on anything else."

"You don't anymore." Dedra's voice was breathy. It was hard to speak with her stomach tied up in such excited knots. This time, when she tilted her chin up, she was rewarded with Andrés' kiss.

Soft but firm, his lips met hers, and she felt herself melt into him. Their tongues met, embracing in a moment she'd been waiting for. A moment she worried might not stand up to her hopes, but right then proved that she had nothing to worry about.

Andrés was a great kisser.

But before they could go any further, Andrés

pulled back. "We need food. If I don't go get it now, we'll starve tonight."

"No room service at the compound?" she asked, refusing to let him out of her embrace just yet.

"Nope." Andrés leaned forward and kissed her again, shorter this time but just as passionate. "But that's what I'm here for."

She couldn't deny that she was hungry, and it would be good to have plenty of strength if they wanted to have lots of fun that night. "Hurry back," she told him, holding on to his hand as he walked away, only letting go of his fingers at the last second.

It wasn't fair. Such a tease!

As the door shut behind him, she pulled herself together.

She was a grown-ass woman who'd waited two days already. She could get through dinner without jumping him!

She sighed and turned to survey the room. It was full of amenities to keep even the fussiest guests feeling pampered. She was especially pleased to see the large soaking tub, complete with some bottles of bubble bath along the edge. With nothing else to do, she decided to indulge herself.

By the time Andrés returned with a chilled bottle of champagne and a few takeout containers, Dedra was well into her soak. She'd pinned most of her hair back but for the few strands that refused to stay put.

She heard him groan—a sexy sound—when he approached her. "How am I supposed to eat a hamburger when something like this is waiting for me?"

She made a face. "Burgers, really?" It wasn't the sexiest food. She couldn't help but visualize a hunk of ground meat falling into the tub as she ate.

"Then how will sushi do?" he asked, revealing a container full of it. "I promise it's good. We have so many pescatarians here that our cafeteria has to get it right."

Dedra smiled as he located a tray that fit perfectly across the bathtub and then placed the container with a pair of chopsticks on it. Sushi was much sexier to eat and had the added bonus of not making her feel bloated afterward!

"I got some exotic fruits for dessert." He showed her another container.

"How about you pop that in the mini fridge. I have a feeling we'll be ravenous later." She accepted the glass of champagne from him and clinked his glass when he offered it.

"To a successful mission."

"To our new friendship," she added.

They both took a sip, and then he raised an eyebrow. "Just friendship?"

When their food was eaten and Andrés had cleared the containers away, she turned on the hot water, not that she thought they'd need help warming it up.

Then she cocked a finger. She didn't have to do any more.

They kissed. Her body was warm, pink from the water, yet it was his kiss that made her feel flushed. "Am I getting out, or are you coming in?"

"I think I'd be missing out if I didn't get to swim with the goose."

"Then gently peel your designer garments off that modelesque physique and let me properly admire those tanned, taut abs again."

He did as she instructed, and she took a slow sip of her champagne while looking at him from head to tip.

Stopping at the tip. Licking her lips.

He sauntered closer, and closer, until his cock, standing at attention, was right at level with her face.

She reached for him, running a finger along his shaft, moving her eyes between the magnificent cock and his eyes full of lust. She coaxed him forward until she could lean enough to lick the tip. He pushed closer, letting her lips close around him, and groaned when the champagne bubbles surprised him.

She continued, swallowing the champagne and starting to really use her tongue. She loved having a man like this, having the power to bring him so much pleasure. Especially with a cock like Andrés'—long, thick, hard, and smooth. She'd perfected this technique long ago and knew she could get the result she wanted.

But he wasn't going to let her. He pulled back and removed the bathtub tray. She pulled the drain plug, letting some of the water out before he got in and overflowed it.

Then he was in the tub with her, coming in behind her so her back was leaned against him. God help her if it wasn't the sexiest, most comfortable feeling she'd had in some time. She rested against his chest, feeling his shaft pressed longways up her back while his hands roamed her body, caressing her breasts before moving lower. He teased her to start, running his hands along her inner thighs before finally exploring the jackpot.

He kissed her neck while fingers on one hand worked her clit like a master and the other hand cupped her breast. Dedra couldn't remember the last time she'd been played like a fine instrument, but to her delight, Andrés was quickly working her to a crescendo.

"You should stop if you don't want me to come," she whispered in his ear.

"Why wouldn't I want you to have multiple orgasms tonight, my sexy Dedra?" His voice was nearly a sexy growl and all she needed to push her over the edge.

Dedra let herself get caught up in it, let the pleasure explode from her body, all while Andrés' strong arms held her tight and his fingers gently slowed.

They were silent and still for a moment. With her eyes closed, Dedra enjoyed Andrés' embrace, took in his sexy masculine smell, and let him press his lips to her temple.

She sighed.

"You're magnificent," he whispered.

"Back atcha," she replied, opening her eyes and turning her head to kiss him. She was ready for more.

Turning her body, she wrapped her arms around him to pull him close and deepen their kiss. To her surprise, he stood, pulling her up in his arms.

"What are you doing?" she squealed. "We're going to get water everywhere."

"Not if you help me." He nodded his head, and she saw that he indicated the fluffy robes within arm's reach. Since his arms were full, holding her, she grabbed them.

"What do you want me to do?" he asked, "I'm not taking a step until you tell me exactly what you want."

"I want you to take me to that bed." Her voice was even huskier than before.

Andrés followed her directions, barely waiting for her to throw the robes down before he placed her on top of them and began kissing down her body. He stopped at each nipple, giving them both a swirl of his tongue and a gentle nip before he started kissing lower. He went down her stomach, and then one hip, then down the leg…

"You just pleased me," Dedra gasped. "Andrés, it's my turn to pleasure you."

He kissed back up her other leg, not yet kissing her sex, instead making his way back up her hip, then stomach, then back to the nipples before he pulled back just a bit. "This is my pleasure." The way his eyes bore into hers with intense passion made her catch her breath. He was so damn sexy, and everything about the way he smiled promised that he meant what he said. "You let me worship your body, and I'm getting plenty out of it. Every time my name spills off that tongue, it's an extra jolt. Trust me."

In a swift move, he pushed her up the bed so her head rested comfortably on the pillows and spread her legs apart, guiding her knees to drop to either side so he could dip his head and treat her to a long, slow lick over her sex.

She couldn't help but cry out, it felt so good. He tightened his grip on one of her knees a bit, to let her know he enjoyed hearing it.

Despite the fact that she was enjoying herself, and he was enjoying what he was doing to her, Dedra couldn't take it anymore. She barely felt like she was over the first orgasm, and he was about to give her another.

She laced her hands in his hair and begged him to fuck her. When he took a moment to stop and smile up at her, she took her chance, sliding out from his hold.

"Aww, is playtime over?" he asked, that damn dimple appearing again.

She kissed the little notch by his smile. "Get on your back."

He smiled even bigger and, once again, did as told. He paused for a second, reaching over to the side table for a box.

Dedra was glad one of them was thinking. Not that it was very likely she'd get pregnant, but it seemed like a good common courtesy to extend when you hadn't had the STD talk yet.

He tossed her one, and she gladly opened the wrapper and placed the rubber on his tip. She cupped his balls with the other hand and made sheathing him into a mini hand job. His eyes rolled back as she did it, and she saw what he meant about it being pleasurable to hear the other person moan.

"Are you ready?" Dedra asked him, moving one leg to the other side so she was straddling him.

"Fuck yeah," Andrés said as Dedra slid him into her. She did it slowly, wanting to enjoy the first moments of feeling him inside of her. Then she began to move.

His hips rocked with hers, and his hands reached up to her breasts. Soon they were moving faster, and Dedra had to lean over and prop herself up with the headboard.

When Andrés was close, he moved a hand between them, massaging her clit to bring her over the edge with him. Dedra soared as his hips bucked under her, gazing into the eyes of this truly amazing man.

It was just the first of several rounds they had that night.

Dedra had hoped Andrés would be good in the bedroom, but he was even better than she could have dreamed.

7

Dedra always woke when a text came in. The little chime and buzz broke through any sleep, much like her baby's crying had twenty years earlier.

She hoped it was Kailee letting her know that their plane had landed and they'd be to the academy soon. She couldn't wait to see her.

Andrés was asleep, so she took the phone to the bathroom, where the light and sounds wouldn't bother him. He'd been so good to her, not just last night but over the last two days. A part of Dedra was always waiting for the other shoe to drop, to find out that the person she was into had issues, like Rod's gambling, but so far, Andrés had been great. Sure, she didn't know much about his personal life, or even his professional life, past working for FUC academy, but something about him felt different than other men she'd dated. Maybe when things were right, you just knew.

She saw Kailee had sent her a photo and opened it, expecting a cute selfie. Maybe she'd even have that handsome young agent in it with her.

Instead, the image that loaded made Dedra's blood run cold.

It was only half of Kailee's face but enough for Dedra to see that her daughter was gagged. The main focus of the photo was the background, which Dedra recognized immediately.

The factory.

Along with the photo was one line.

Get here now.

She frantically typed out a text, demanding to know who had Kailee, who was sending this to her, and what the hell they wanted. When she hit Send, she was treated to an alert message.

This user has blocked you.

"Son of a bitch!" As soon as Dedra shouted it, she covered her mouth. She didn't want to wake up Andrés. She peeked out into the room and saw he hadn't moved. So far, she'd played by FUC rules. She'd arrived here, and she'd been convinced her daughter was safe. Now, she had no idea what had happened to Kailee's agent, how these assholes had gotten ahold of her daughter, but she was going to handle it herself.

She'd tried doing it the FUC way, and that had clearly failed. FUC or not, they had nothing on Dedra Goosby-Wakins, mob princess.

Dedra was shaking with rage. The only person she debated talking to was Grayson, but if they wanted her brother or nephew, they would have delivered them messages. Grayson had been out of the business for so long he wasn't their target. Dedra was.

She'd tried to hold on to the factory, to bring it around, to make it something Grayson would want to be a part of. Even Kailee, who never had any interest in it, could have come around. But none of that mattered. She'd burn the whole thing to the ground if that was what they wanted, so long as it meant she could keep them from harming her daughter.

She turned off the bathroom light and snuck into the bedroom. As quietly as she could, she dressed then shoved a few things into her purse. She resisted the urge to kiss Andrés. He was just so damn sexy, but she knew enough about him to know he'd want to stick to the rules. He'd hear what happened and pull the whole FUC team out of bed, and then they'd sit there in another meeting while *those people* had her precious Kailee.

She spared one last glance at him, thinking of how much a shame it was that they couldn't have more time together. She'd rather enjoyed him. But she decided to look at it like one last fun time before she met her end.

Because she would die for Kailee, if it came to that.

She made her way through the building and down to the basement, where Andrés had parked his truck. She'd made sure to grab the keys out of his pants pocket. She felt a little guilty for it, but it wasn't really even his truck. It was a FUC-issued staff vehicle. So really, she was stealing from FUC.

After all they've done for me...

Sure, they'd gone out of their way to bring her back here, but look at how they'd also failed! They delivered only three out of four Goosby family members, and seventy-five percent was a fail, as far as Dedra was concerned.

She thought about trying to disable the GPS, but it really didn't matter. As soon as they knew she was gone, they'd figure out where she'd gone. All that mattered was that she got Kailee out safe. She'd meet whatever terms her *employees*—she hated thinking of them that way; her employees were people she cared about—and MUFF made. FUC be damned.

She felt slightly bad for the factory employees who hadn't been a part of this. If the factory went down, they'd be out of a job. Didn't the dissenters understand that? She took solace in the fact that they had good benefits packages. They'd be taken care of for some time while they looked for new employment.

Dedra unlocked the truck and got in. She started the engine. Would the guard let her pass, or would she have to drive through the gate? Maybe it was automatic...

The thoughts had taken just enough extra time to put a crimp in her plans, because, just then, the passenger door opened.

"Hello, *Xuxu*."

Andrés.

Andrés was wiser than to ask her where she was going while she was packing her things.

It even amused him when she went into his pants and took his keys.

It would have been asking her to lie to him or starting an argument if he let her know he was awake. If she wanted him to know what she was doing, she would have told him.

So he lay still in bed, watching this wonderful woman leave him.

He would have been sad to see her go if he hadn't been planning on following right behind her.

He knew that Dedra was trying to escape. He just didn't know if she'd planned this all along or if something had changed her mind. He'd seen her take her phone into the bathroom. He wondered if she'd gotten a message.

As soon as she was gone, Andrés took out his phone, tapped a message to Alyce, and followed Dedra.

He watched her go straight to his staff vehicle and stealthily made his way through the garage, drawing a little extra on his ocelot to help with it. It would be best if he could get into the car without her noticing. It meant not risking getting run over.

"Hello, *xuxu*." He greeted his sexy lady, Dedra, as he sat in the passenger's seat.

He laughed when she jumped. He met her glare when she turned to him, and he saw she pressed her hand to her heart from being startled. "What the fuck, Andrés?"

"Figured you could use some adrenaline. You were sure taking your time to get into gear." He motioned to the stick. "You can drive manual, right?"

"Of course I can! I was just wondering if I should have killed you before I left so I wouldn't have to deal with shit like this!"

"I'm pretty sure you were just thinking you would miss me." He leaned over and kissed her cheek. "Now, tell me where we're going, and why."

Not wasting any more time, Dedra threw the car into reverse, letting the tires squeal as she turned out of the parking space and headed out of the underground garage. "They have my daughter."

8

Kailee was sure her mom was going to kill someone.

Maybe everyone.

Starting with the factory workers. No, scratch that, she bet her mom would take out the cultists first then take her time in making Jimmy and the others pay.

It wasn't about the paychecks or sick days or bonuses. That was what every boss gave their employees. For Dedra Wakins, it was about how the workers were like family. It was about the Christmas company parties, the spring field days, the "bring your kids to work" days. The time they'd spent over the years getting to know each other and their families. Their spouses, their kids. Theirs was a small town, and the people who worked there often stayed there. Which meant some had seen Dedra grow up. They'd all seen Kailee grow up. They were like aunts and uncles.

And now they'd betrayed Dedra and Kailee.

The revolt was one thing, but laying hands on her daughter?

They were fucked.

Kailee felt confident in that, but it wasn't enough to keep away any trepidation. She knew from the moment they took out her FUC agent that the MUFF cultists had no regard for anyone but themselves.

Although she hadn't been privy to any of her grandfather's business, and she had no idea how much or little participation her mom might have had in mob activities, Kailee was sure she knew one thing about that lifestyle: even the biggest criminal should follow some code of honor. And that usually meant not getting kids involved and giving a man a chance to bargain before taking his life.

They'd killed her FUC agent in cold blood, with no regard for any rules or any code.

Kailee tried to change her thoughts. She couldn't think about her FUC agent. She didn't even want to think his name. She couldn't lose her composure at a time like this. She had to stay focused and try to figure out how to escape her little storage room prison.

Her hands were tied behind her with zip ties—which she sure as shit knew how to snap out of, thanks to her mother's early training—but a cultist sat in the room with her at all times. She knew there was another in the hallway, having passed that one when Pauline came by to escort her to the bathroom —a luxury she got because the cultists said they didn't want to have to stand watch in a room that had a crap corner.

She was as furious with Pauline as she was with Jimmy, but she could also tell Pauline felt bad. She'd been sneaking Kailee food and apologizing, but she swore she was unable to help in any other way.

Kailee knew she could save herself by shifting into her narwhal form if she ran out of other options. She highly doubted that they knew she could do that. It was risky, though, and had to be a last resort.

It wasn't whether or not she could shift out of water—she knew she could do that. Her father once told her that every young marine mammal experimented with land shifts before they accepted how uncomfortable it was. The problem she faced was how much energy it took to be in that form when you didn't have the water to help support the weight of the medium-sized whale. Which made the whole thing uncomfortable, to say the least.

And while shifting would crush anyone in her immediate vicinity, she'd be pretty helpless against any other armed people who rushed from other areas. Narwhals on land didn't have offensive capabilities, and as a female narwhal, she didn't even have a huge horn to thrash around.

It's not even a horn; it's a tooth, she muttered to herself, to the tune of sour grapes.

So she'd have to shift, crush her captors, shift back into human form as fast as possible, and hope she still had enough energy to bolt from pursuers.

Which was why she was holding off on it until she had no other options.

For now, she'd wait and see if they decided to make demands that she could meet.

It was then that Jimmy came into her holding room. He exchanged some words with the cultist, who then patted him down and left.

The sight of Jimmy infuriated her, but Kailee was also confused. "Why the pat down? I thought you were all on the same team."

Jimmy approached her then crouched down. She could see a sadness in his face, but she refused to fall for it. He sighed before telling her, "I'm sorry, Kailee. This wasn't supposed to happen. They weren't supposed to touch you. You have to understand that I had no idea."

Jimmy was one of the older factory workers, one who had seen her when she was just a newborn being carried around by Dedra. Hell, he probably even came to the house to the baby viewing party after she was born. *This asshole!* "I don't get this at all, Jimmy. If you were so unhappy, why go this far? Why not just quit? Why not take the benefits package available to anyone who wanted out?"

Jimmy shoved his hand into his hair, pulling at it and making the dark grey strands stand out in all different directions. He got up and started pacing the small space. "I don't know. It's like this idea got in my head somewhere, and everywhere I looked, there were articles about gentrification and deindustrialization, that kind of shit that talks about how the whole world is changing and no one gives a shit about people like me anymore. I got carried away with the stuff."

Were she not tied up and kidnapped, Kailee might have allowed herself to comfort Jimmy. But this buffoon should have reached out before starting a riot and invited a dangerous group of cultists to bring it to another level.

One thing struck her about what he said, though. As an internet influencer—the preferred term to "socialite" since she did more than go to parties, she also posted photos on Instagram!—she knew a lot about how algorithms, bots, and trolls worked. Was someone targeting Jimmy with this message? "Where are you seeing this stuff, Jimmy? On the news? In the paper?"

He shook his head. "Social media, mostly, but also sometimes email. Like, junk emails, addresses I don't know, but I can't help but read them, and they talk about the dangers of change."

"And the others? Were they seeing this stuff?"

"Yeah!" Jimmy turned back to her, animated. "That's how we all got wound up about it. We'd come into work and had all seen the same thing, and we all got to bitching about it all day long. Then that night, we see another one, go back to work, and do it all again."

Kailee nodded, tucking the fact away, as it wouldn't do her any good right then. "I just don't get how you got from reading articles to getting a *cult* involved."

"I don't know. I just got the video, and it had the

number, and I just acted. I never really thought about how bad it could be." He looked back at her. "You have to know I'm sorry."

She didn't know he was sorry. Didn't care. "Video?" she asked, ignoring his pseudo-apology.

She listened, horrified, as Jimmy explained the video, how he'd gotten it, and what was on it. Kailee knew her mom wouldn't have been on video in a field shifting. She only did it on private property or when completely alone. Hell, even when she was in hotel rooms, she always stayed in places that had automatic checkout and windows that opened!

"And the number on the video was to MUFF? And you called them and invited them to help you without figuring out exactly how unhinged they were?"

Jimmy nodded, putting his face in his hands. "I know I really screwed the pooch on this one. I've been trying to figure out how to get you out of here, but I can't get by them."

"Are they armed?" she asked.

He nodded and uttered a muffled *uh-huh.*

"You understand that they probably want to kill my mom, right?" If the way they'd dispatched Kailee's FUC agent was any indication of how little regard they gave to human life. "Is that what you wanted?"

"No!" Jimmy shouted, bringing himself to meet her gaze. "We just wanted to raise a stink to get her here and get her to agree to bring back the old machines."

"That's stupid," Kailee said. "You know your co-workers like the machines, right? These new models make it easier for them to work." Her mother had told her plenty, and she'd also seen the responses on social media.

"I don't fucking know what I was thinking, okay?" Jimmy punched the wall, causing Kailee to jump in her chair.

She realized she might be giving Jimmy too much trust. Maybe he was just as unhinged as the cultists. She decided to change her tactic, allowing her fear to show a bit and taking on a softer, more vulnerable tone. "Jimmy, I believe you. I want to, at least."

He shook his head and then brought his fist to his lips, as though that would help with the pain. "Yeah?"

Kailee nodded. "Yeah, just call my mom, okay? Let her know what's going on, what part of the factory I'm in, how many cultists, whatever you know about the plan."

"How am I supposed to call your mom? You got her number?"

No. Of course not. Kailee had never memorized a phone number, except her own cell phone. "MUFF has my phone. Can't you get it from them? The number is in there."

"Sure. Like that wouldn't be suspicious. And you think I haven't already thought about this? I even went to your mom's secretary, and she blew me off because she said your mom is on holiday and no one gets to contact her."

He was right. "When she finds out I'm missing, she'll know something is wrong and come here. You have to meet up with her and let her know what's going on." It was a last-ditch effort, the last thing she could think of. Jimmy had been getting closer to the door, and Kailee knew that she was out of luck.

"I would, but it's not going to help if she kills me first because she knows I'm part of this or if the cultists are watching me and take me or her out when I try to intercept. I'm sorry, Kailee. There's nothing I can do."

9

They drove through the night, past sunrise, until Dedra finally saw the Goosby factory come into view.

"Did they say 'come alone' in their message?" Andrés asked.

"No. They didn't say anything other than get here." Her pulse thudded in her ears as she thought about Kailee, inside that building with some creepy strangers. She hoped her daughter hadn't been hurt. She hoped everything would be okay.

"Of course not. They don't consider us a threat. Or the cops or anyone. They're full of themselves, and that overconfidence is always the undoing of a villain." He reached over and took her hand, much to her comfort. "Come on. Let's go get your daughter."

"Why are you doing this? Why aren't you waiting for the whole FUC team?" She was grateful that he was there with her, but it didn't make sense, based on what she knew of Andrés. He'd been such a good agent when they were flying. Why would he change his ways now?

"I sent them a message, but I knew it was better for me to be here with you than it was to let you go off on your own or to try to make you wait for the team to assemble."

"Even if you get in trouble with FUC over it?"

He reached over and took her hand, taking his eyes off the road momentarily to look at her. "I wouldn't risk it for just anyone. You're something else, Dedra. I want to be here with you."

She squeezed his hand in thanks. "I just hope Kailee's okay."

"If your daughter's half as savvy as you, which I'm sure she is because her mamma raised her right, then she's holding her own, and we're just going to swoop in and get her out."

As Andrés pulled the car into the parking lot, Dedra saw that it was full of employee vehicles. That wouldn't normally be surprising, as it was a weekday, but Dedra had expected the factory to be emptied by the dissenting workers and MUFF.

It put a snag in her plans. "I don't want innocent people to get hurt," Dedra told Andrés. "I thought we'd just be going in to face off with MUFF. We'll need to evacuate."

Andrés parked the car. "But we'll need a cover story so the public doesn't ask questions about why the factory shut down for the day. We can say someone reported bedbugs or something."

"*Bedbugs?!*" Dedra screeched. "Are you trying to get us shut down forever?! You can't tell the public that a bedding factory has *bedbugs!*" She'd rather burn the place to the ground than let the public think they had parasites!

"Whoa, hold on, okay?" Andrés held up his hands in front of him, as though protecting his eyes in case she turned goose and started pecking. "How about we say a small fire then?"

She sighed and forced herself to stop glaring at him. "Fine, let's go." She directed him to the administrative entrance.

"They probably have people watching." She looked at him, wondering how obvious it was that she'd brought a special agent with her.

She didn't think it looked obvious at all. Andrés looked like a normal cowboy. Nice ass-hugging jeans, plaid flannel shirt. Nothing 007 secret-agenty about him.

Nothing obviously shifter-like either, which was good. MUFF knew she was a goose, and that meant they might think Andrés was too. That would let his scrappy feline side have a bit of an edge if it came down to it.

Anyone observing them would likely think that Andrés was no one to worry about. Just her current boyfriend.

Boyfriend.

But was he? She couldn't help wonder as they walked into the building together. He wasn't here on FUC orders. He was there for her. He'd said she was special. She felt the same way about him. Like this could be something long-term if they both wanted it to be.

But did she? After Norbert died, she thought she'd spend the rest of her life alone. Sure, she had diversions, like Rod, but she never thought she'd connect with someone.

But she felt she was connecting with Andrés. Like he was a kindred spirit.

Maybe it was just her imagination, but she thought Andrés' determination to take down the bad guys and save Kailee matched her own level of intensity. Like he cared because she cared.

And they felt like a team. It was something she might be able to get used to with Andrés.

If they got out of this alive.

Still not knowing what to expect—but reasoning that MUFF and company would at least want to talk before they shot—they made their way through the factory. The place felt like home to Dedra. Really, she'd known this place her whole life, versus the house she currently resided in, which had been for only the last ten years.

And someone is daring to try to fuck with it.

She was fearful for Kailee and wanted to figure out where she was right away, but she knew she couldn't make any wrong moves that might set them off and get her daughter hurt. So they went to the main office area first.

"Dedra! Hey." Her assistant, Betsy, greeted her. "We didn't expect you—"

Dedra cut her off. "I know. I'm back on some issues. Is everything okay here?" It was looking like a regular working day, except for the fact that Betsy was blaring a KPOP station that Dedra didn't normally allow on—or at that volume.

"Yeah, so far as I know." Betsy turned down her music then seemed to remember. "Oh, I did hear some noise about Jimmy and a few other of your dad's best workers raising a stink but nothing worth calling you back from vacation."

That was good news. It meant that people weren't being harmed and no real damage was being done. "How many of them? And what are the other workers saying?"

"Um, three that I know of, I think. Oh, and yesterday a few others started walking around all creepy-like in black robes. I don't even know who they are. Security was going to ask them to leave today, but we were giving them time to just get it out of their system and leave on their own. Ignoring them because it's like they're daring us to do something so they can act out, you know?" Betsy shrugged and scrunched up her face, as though saying, *what can you do?*

Dedra thought it was probably good that security, or other employees, hadn't confronted any of them about it. That might have triggered them to violence. She exchanged a look with Andrés. "Betsy, I'm back because some stuff is going on, and it's all going to be fine, but I need everyone to go home today."

Betsy's face paled. "We'd lose a whole day of productivity."

Dedra pursed her lips together and nodded. "I know, but I want to make sure everyone is safe."

The assistant balked even more. "What's going on?"

Andrés covered for her. "The city is looking into some potential blockage in the area, just some sewer cleanup, but it might be stinky. Not a safety problem at all."

Dedra was impressed at the story. "Just call out the non-hazardous evacuation code to send everyone home, okay?"

Betsy still looked suspicious but did as she was told, picking up her phone and using the internal comm system to call out the announcement.

While she did, Dedra turned to her locked office door, punching in her code and using the palm-print ID panel to let herself in. She closed her door behind her while she accessed her safe. Inside, she found her loaded gun, a spare burner phone that was fully charged, and an old paper address book. Turning to the desk, she found a few numbers in the book to save on the phone. Then she tucked the gun into her waistband and the phone in her bra and returned the book to the safe.

In the reception area, she saw Betsy was already gone. Andrés was facing the window. She followed his gaze to see the stream of people heading to their cars. "Seems like you tell people to go home and they don't dawdle."

"Of course not." Dedra wondered what kind of jobs Andrés had had in his life if he was surprised by the speed in which people would go to play hooky.

When the trail of staff leaving the building dwindled, Betsy's phone rang. "Hello," Dedra said into the speakerphone, holding back from shouting, *Give me my fucking daughter back, you fucking walking corpses.*

"You've made it here. Good." Dedra didn't recognize the voice.

"What the hell is this about?" Dedra asked. "Where is my daughter? What do you want from us?"

"You're going to bring back the geese," the voice said.

"What?" Dedra tried to wrap her head around the words.

"The geese. You fired them all. Where are they? We demand they be reinstated."

"What?" Dedra asked again, her brain trying to wrap around what was being said. "The geese? I don't have any geese." *The fuck?*

"That's bullshit. Your company bragged about

your specially engineered Canadian goose down. *Your* goose down."

That was true in so far as they'd used specific farmers and bred them for generations. But they were no longer being bred. "They've all been placed on nice farms to rest out their days."

"You better hope that farm isn't a euphemism for murder!" the voice hissed at her.

"It's not. They've literally been re-homed on farms." She shook her head and shrugged to Andrés and saw he looked as confused as she felt.

"Farms where they'll be eaten!" The voice turned shrill.

"No... they're much too old for that, and geese aren't a common table item." Pushing her confusion aside, she cross-referenced the number on the caller ID to the factory directory, figuring out that they were in the main floor supervisor's office.

"And once they die, then what? Too bad, geese? You think because you're a shifter, you're the only one who matters?"

"Do you not understand that the geese weren't employees, shedding their feathers year after year? They were bred, yes, but each year they were, um *used*. Get it?" Dedra couldn't understand what their problem was.

"All that matters is that they lived! And now you're not breeding them anymore, which means they're gone! But no matter. They'll be brought back to their righteous glory once we kill you and your daughter. The factory will be ours, and *we* will reinstate the geese, ensuring their proper value to mankind is preserved and they never have to worry about extinction again."

The caller hung up. Dedra looked at Andrés and shook her head. "What in the actual *fuck?*"

10

Andrés walked with Dedra down to the main factory floor. Now that the factory was empty, they felt they were able to seek out the cultists and dissenters.

"Yeah, MUFF is a little bit… different," he told her. "But that doesn't mean they're not dangerous. Quite the opposite. They can get wound up and do terrible things without thinking first."

"Then we'll have to get them first."

He liked the cold rage look on her, but he just hoped that meant she would think before she acted. They didn't need both sides going off.

As they walked through the doorway of the main floor, Andrés saw figures moving from the opposite end, toward them. "Any idea why they think that killing you would let them have control of the company?"

"No," Dedra answered. "But I would shoot them right now if I knew Kailee would be okay."

"You're packing?" He'd wondered if that was what she'd done when she went into her office.

"Yeah. Aren't you?" she replied.

"Of course." And plenty of other tricks up his sleeve.

"Here she is, destroyer of non-sentient geese!" one of the black-robed figures leading the group called out. As they got closer, Andrés got a good look at his face and identified him from the mission file. His name was Brain.

Beside Brain was another black-cloaked figure. The group also had two plain-clothed men, a plain-clothed woman, and a blonde who had to be Kailee, being held by the third black-robed person.

"And here he is, the biggest living dummy I've ever seen," Dedra replied, seeming absolutely fearless, though Andrés saw that her eyes were locked on Kailee.

The girl, who could have been a clone of her mother, looked unharmed and, if anything, annoyed. Andrés laughed to himself. The resemblance wasn't just in the platinum hair; it was also in the way they both looked like they wanted to beat some MUFF.

"Don't bother, Mom," Kailee called out, her voice steady and confident. "These ding-dongs don't understand that the geese are better off now that they aren't being bred to be plucked!"

"They're out of jobs! They served an important purpose in building up this country, and now you're trying to wipe them out of history!" The woman MUFF member, Vergie, if Andrés remembered correctly, reached out and smacked Kailee across the face.

Everything fell apart then. It seemed to happen in slow motion. Andrés saw the woman closest to Kailee and Vergie—she wasn't in a robe so she must be a factory worker—shove Vergie one way and Kailee the other, away from the group. Vergie and the factory worker struggled to one side, but Andrés saw Kailee get a safe distance away.

At the same time, Dedra pulled her gun, but with both figures on the ground, she didn't have a target to shoot.

At the sight of Dedra's gun, Brain and Elon, the other cultist, pulled out their weapons...

But Andrés had to do a double-take to process what the fools were wielding.

Brain had a huge, rusty medieval sword, and Elon, a flail. Brain shouted while pointing his sword at Dedra, circling her as though he was readying for attack. "Animals shouldn't be replaced by non-natural fibers. We want the geese treated humanely, and putting them all out of jobs isn't fair!"

"I swear to the fucking goose god," Dedra muttered, looking at Andrés. "I knew these guys were out there, but this is more birdbrained than I'd anticipated. Do we just kill them?"

Before he could answer, there was a commotion in the air. *Shit!*

A larger-than-normal goose was flying at them then circling above them, squawking, kicking heads, hitting faces with his wings, and shitting as well.

At least most of it got on the MUFFs.

"Lenny, wise Lenny! We've got her for you! We'll get her to sign over the factory, and your will shall be done!" Brain dropped his sword then followed it to the ground, genuflecting for the bird that had literally shit on him.

Dedra shot a fist in the air and grabbed the thing by its neck. Andrés had no idea how she'd been able to do it without getting injured.

"Look at you! You hurt geese!" Brain screamed at her, following it with a maniacal laugh. "We have proof! Our mission has been fruitful!" Andrés knew that Brain was referring to the MUFF mandate that they bring back proof of atrocities against non-sentient animals or face punishment by their leader.

"That's not a goose. That's my uncle Lenny!" Dedra shouted. He could see the fury pooling in her cheeks.

The stupid thing quacked.

"Clearly it's a goose!" Brain proclaimed, motioning with wide-open arms.

While they fought, Andrés fiddled with some items he always kept stashed in his pocket. A paper-clip. A rubber band. This and that.

"Lenny, I will shoot you if you don't change right now!" Dedra still held the gun on Brain but gave Lenny a good yank and a mean side-eye that suggested she might make good on her promise.

With everyone focused on Dedra and Lenny, Andrés took his chance, using his pocket slingshot, and one of his favorite little potions, and launching first one then the other.

He made contact with the hilt of the sword and the handle of the flail, where the cultists both held on. Neither noticed the projectiles coming at them, but they sure noticed when the liquid from the vials started expanding.

It was a special concoction that Andrés was particularly proud of. When it touched metal, it made it brittle so it would shatter. If it touched flesh, it would envelop it like handcuffs.

He pulled out two rocks next, sending those to the primed weapons, and gleefully watched both medieval weapons fall to pieces, much to the cultists' horror.

The two of them were unarmed and unable to wield their weapons, and the third in the back had been knocked out when the factory worker got the better of her. Andrés turned to Dedra and Lenny.

"Shit, Andrés, that was pretty damn cool." Dedra's compliment was music to his ears, but they didn't have time yet to celebrate.

Another item he liked to keep on him was a little Jones family concoction. "This will help." He dumped the white powder from the tiny vial into his hand and then blew the powder into Lenny's face.

Dedra dropped Lenny as the goose coughed, choked, then transformed into a very ugly, hairy, naked human.

Andrés monitored the group very closely. The MUFF members were aware of shifters, most *were* shifters, but the dissenting factory workers' reactions varied from shock to nausea.

The group all shouted their displeasure.

"What the hell is this!"

"How dare you deceive us!"

"You've been torturing human geese?"

"This shit just wanted the inheritance." Dedra nodded toward her uncle, who was quivering on the floor and holding his hands up in surrender.

It was over.

Dedra saw the way the MUFF cultists looked at her uncle, now realizing that they'd been used as pawns in an ongoing family feud.

Lenny was a bastard son that her grandfather had allowed into the family, but he'd never overcome his jealousy of Dedra's father, the "legitimate" child, and long ago, he'd divulged family information to a rival family.

Lenny had been lucky then that Dedra's grandfather only disowned and disinherited him.

He'd managed to get the video of Dedra shifting because he knew the family spots. Who knew how long he'd been stalking her and waiting to get that footage to use against her?

Kailee informed them that she'd learned that

someone—Lenny—had been anonymously sending the factory workers articles over email and social media. The articles were false and meant to trigger fear and had done the trick.

Once he planted that seed and saw the factory workers protesting, he'd sent the video and directed Jimmy to MUFF.

And then he hung out, in his goose form, outside of the factory so they'd take him in and he could witness all of it.

Dedra, Andrés, and Kailee had just finished piecing it all together and getting confirmation from Lenny and MUFF when FUC stormed the factory.

The team was led by a bouncy blonde dressed as Rambo, who rushed in and started shouting orders. Dedra saw that Mason and Viktor were following her orders, along with some other agents Dedra hadn't met.

"Holy shit, that's *the* Miranda?" Kailee asked her, mirroring Dedra's own awe.

"Live and in action," Dedra murmured, wondering if it was too late in her life to pick up some of those kinds of skills.

Dedra heard Andrés filling Mason in and watched Viktor and a few others place cuffs on MUFF. "What do you want to do about them?"

Andrés asked, jerking a finger to the three factory workers.

"I'm not sure." She looked at Kailee. "What do you think?"

"I'm personally wondering if FUC has some sort of placement for folks like these. People who now know a secret but also owe some debt to FUC for causing such trouble that it demanded FUC resources." Dedra wondered if Kailee was thinking about her agent when she said that.

Miranda nodded sharply. "Sure thing, we'll sort all that out. You three, come with me! And don't try anything. You don't want to get chased by a saber-tooth bunny, do you?"

"Are you kidding?" Pearlene asked, looking from Miranda to Dedra.

"Welcome to a whole new world," Dedra said. "It's going to blow your mind."

EPILOGUE

A few days later, Dedra turned off the extra phone and locked it back away in her vault, along with her gun.

She was glad she hadn't had to use either one. The address book her father left her had just a few lifelines left in it. Favors that could be cashed in. Numbers she could call in a real emergency. But once they were gone, they were gone. So she liked saving them, if she could.

They were her safety net, one family inheritance that she couldn't share, and she was glad that the day hadn't progressed far enough that she had to use them.

She would keep them socked away, a reminder that she had people she could turn to still.

She stepped out of her office and saw Andrés.

He wasn't an old family connection like the ones in her address book, but he was someone she could turn to. He was her people now.

He'd told his boss, Alyce, that he wanted to stay around the factory, in case any others had seen the video or might be interested in an uprising. But Dedra knew the truth. He'd told it to her.

He wanted to see what life was like at her side.

"You sure they don't need you back there, teaching MacGyver 101?" She couldn't believe it when she found out it was a real course. She found it even funnier to learn that one of the assignments in the class was *almost* basket weaving. Andrés said you never knew when you'd need one in the field!

"Nah, it's one of the most popular classes. They'll get another professor in, no problem."

"That's good. I want to make sure Kailee takes the course." Dedra smiled to herself.

Kailee had taken a few years post-high school to learn what she wanted to do. And it was this event that had been the catalyst. She was going to take her social media savvy, the skills she'd gained as an influencer on *Instagram*, *YouTube*, and *TikTok*, and become a FUC agent, specializing in new media techniques and surveillance.

Dedra thought it was just perfect.

"Aren't you sad that she'll be an agent and not following in your footsteps?" Andrés asked.

"Nope, because Maddox is very excited to come in and learn the business. He's talking about bamboo and hemp fibers and all sorts of stuff. I told him that he can learn from me, and when I pass over the reins, he's free to do whatever he wants." She was truly excited. Grayson hadn't promised he'd return to help, but she knew that if Maddox was there, Grayson would be close by.

And that was good enough for her.

"Sounds like the boy will fit right in."

"Mmm-hmm. Besides, maybe Kailee will eventually settle down, have kids of her own, and bring them around to learn from Maddox." She had no idea if kids were in Kailee's future goals, but a mother goose could hope to be a grandgoose someday.

"Hmmm, little narwhals running around? I'd love to see that," Andrés said, wrapping his arms around her and nuzzling her neck. "And if Maddox needs any MacGyver training, I'll be here for him."

Dedra reached up, threading her fingers through Andrés' hair. "And how do you feel about yearly trips to South America?"

"Ah, *xuxu*, that's the second-best part of this deal."

She didn't have to ask him what the first best part of the deal was. He'd already told her many times over that she was.

"Aren't you going to get bored?" Dedra asked, pulling from his embrace to take a perch on her desk while she looked at him. He was a man of adventure. Would he really be okay spending so much time in one place while she mentored Maddox and ran the company?

"Not at all," Andrés said.

"You're going to be a househusband?" She lifted an eyebrow. "A kept man?"

"Not at all. I'm thinking about opening a shop. Getting into making some practical field gear. I'll have time to make prototypes that agents can use in the field or different handmade items that take time and experienced craftsmanship to work on."

She saw his eyes glittering with excitement and knew that he really was passionate about the idea. It was good. It meant he wasn't giving it all up for her; he was just choosing to follow another path with her.

"Hmm… experienced craftsmanship…" Dedra reached out and snared him by the shirt, pulling him close and wrapping her legs around him. "I think that's something I could use right about now."

Then she kissed her ocelot man, knowing full well that they both still had tons to teach each other.

Kailee had amends to make.

She'd fooled around and made her agent compromise his morals. He'd slept with his target and had felt guilty.

Then MUFF murdered him.

She was determined to make it up to him. In his memory, she would work for FUC and keep other people safe in his place. Since he couldn't.

Her whole life she'd been hard-headed, strong-willed, and more independent than was good for her. She'd grown up filthy rich and privileged, and it was time to give back. She had to make something of herself, to make up for her mistake, and make sure it never happened again.

So she enrolled in the Furry United Coalition Newbie Academy.

She'd expected to run into some people who didn't want to accept her. Some people who held a grudge against her for her agent's death.

But what she hadn't expected was for him to show up again, alive.

And keeping a doozy of a secret.

Kailee thought her agent was dead, but she'll come to learn that he survived! When they do meet again, they'll both have some secrets. Perhaps unforgiveable ones.

THE END

Not quite! There are more FUC Academy books coming. Bat and the Bone by **ALEXA GREGORY**, plus, **EVE LANGLAIS**, the FUC world creator, has a book coming soon called Panda and the Kitty. And don't forget about the first academy book, **MANDY ROSKO's**, I'll be Dammed, featuring a beaver!

To find out more about these books and more, please visit Worlds.Eve-Langlais.com or stay in the loop with our newsletter - sign up here.

ABOUT THE AUTHOR

Renee Hewett writes short and spicy paranormal romance. She's lived in western New York, central Texas, and Canada (prairies and central). She writes small town contemporary romance as Jessica Ripley. You can sign up for her newsletter at: https://www.subscribepage.com/reneehewett

Learn more at: http://reneehewett.com/